A death dealing prisoner escapes
—the hard way...

The door slid open and a cuss stepped in with a double ten-gauge and blew the prisoner's head to bloody hash!

By that time, of course, Longarm had drawn, fired, and dropped the shotgunner across Amarillo Jack's lap. Then he kicked the door shut again and said, conversationally, "I believe it was *me* you had in mind."

The man he'd shot in the side of the face rolled off to the floor, blowing bloody bubbles and making all sorts of odd noises. Longarm leaned forward to pat him down, removed a derringer from his vest and said, "Shame on you. Just stay put down there and first aid should arrive any day now."

TABOR EVANS

LONGARM

AND THE DOOMED WITNESS

JOVE BOOKS, NEW YORK

LONGARM AND THE DOOMED WITNESS

A Jove Book/published by arrangement with
the author

PRINTING HISTORY
Jove edition/June 1989

ISBN: 0-515-10035-8

Jove Books are published by The Berkley Publishing Group
200 Madison Avenue, New York, New York 10016.
The name "JOVE" and the "J" logo
are trademarks belonging to Jove Publications, Inc.

PRINTED IN THE UNITED STATES OF AMERICA

10 9 8 7 6 5 4 3 2 1

Chapter 1

A bullet through one's hat has a wondrous power to concentrate one's mind. So when Longarm fired back he aimed with malicious intent to deposit Amarillo Jack on the corner of 14th and Larimer with a shattered thighbone and an awesome amount of screaming for a gent who gloried in his rep as a hitherto laconic killer.

Amarillo Jack's sawed-off six-gun now lay two or three feet out of reach, still smoking, on the red sandstone sidewalk its owner was bleeding all over. That was still a mite close for Longarm's taste. So as he joined them on the corner, his own double-action .44-40 in hand, he began by kicking Amarillo Jack over the high granite curb into the somewhat soggy gutter before he hunkered down to pick up the owlhoot's weapon, saying, "Morning, you back-shooting son of a bitch. This old Schofield .45 would have

1

surely done the job on me if it didn't carry a mite high. I've never figured out why Schofields do that, either. You'd think the army would order guns that were sighted better, seeing as they issue so many of 'em. I take it this was the side arm that cavalry officer was packing over to Fort Gibson when you shot him in the back with that piss-ant .38 they have you packing on your Wanted fliers?"

The man sprawled in the gutter with a broken leg kept his teeth clenched lest he scream as he replied, "Go ahead an' get it over with, Longarm. I'm hurting like hell and the horseshit down here smells dreadful, besides."

Longarm chuckled fondly down at Amarillo Jack to assure him, "Had I wanted you dead I'd have aimed a mite higher. Just you take it easy and the meat wagon will be along directly to carry you to County General. They do things up to date in Denver these days. What with gas street lamps and other wonders of modern science they may even save that leg for you. I sure hope so. For hanging a one-legged man does sound sort of cruel and unusual, and I've taken an oath to uphold the Constitution as a federal lawman, you know."

The wanted killer he'd shot and deposited in the gutter turned a sicker shade of green but managed a last ounce of defiance as he made a most unpleasant remark about Longarm's mother and added, "Go on and get it over with, damn your eyes! You know how many of your fellow lawmen I've kilt and I'd have done you the same, just now, had I took more time to aim!"

Longarm smiled thinly and replied, "That surely would have messed up my weekend. The paperwork they put me through each time I put one of

2

you old boys away for keeps can slow me down almost as bad, and the lady who's expecting me to come calling as soon as I get off early this fine Saturday doesn't like to be kept waiting. So just hold on and...where in thunder could the infernal Denver P.D. be hiding out on us in broad-ass day?"

As if that had been his stage cue, a blue-uniformed member of the local police force stuck a head around the brick corner of a nearby building, took in the scene at a glance, and felt free to expose himself further, saying, "Morning, Longarm. I might have known it was you disturbing the peace in for-God's-sake-downtown Denver during business hours. What have we got here?"

Longarm finished reloading and put his six-gun back in its cross-draw rig under his tobacco tweed frock coat as he told the copper-badge, "They call it Amarillo Jack. It's a fitting name when you consider Amarillo means yellow, in Mex. He just tried to back-shoot me on my way to work at the Federal Building. Before that, he's been known to treat other lawmen even meaner. He seems to have a natural resentment for authority."

The copper-badge moved closer, gazed down into the gutter, and whistled softly before he said, "We've had some fliers on this rabid hound. It's funny, he don't *look* like my picture of a total lunatic. How come you didn't finish him off and save Colorado the expense of a trial and hanging, Longarm?"

The taller and more experienced federal deputy didn't want to discuss the morals of a certain widow woman up on Sherman Avenue. So he just said, "I'm sure the federal government will pay his local medical expenses. Fort Smith, Arkansas, will likely get stuck for the rope and pine box he'll require once he's up and around again. Old Jack, here, back-shot way more lawmen in the Cherokee Strip than he ever managed to back-shoot here in Colorado. I busted his fool leg as a courtesy to old George Maledon, Judge Parker's hangman. Business over yonder has been sort of slow of late and old George has hardly any other source of income."

The usually busy intersection, cleared by the dulcet tones of gunplay, was coming back to life once more as folk who'd ducked into doorways, down behind watering troughs and such began to either go on about their business or drift over for a look-see at the downed owlhoot. Then, fortunately, the mule-drawn ambulance from County General hove into view before anyone in the crowd could really piss on the groaning casualty in the gutter. When the copper-badge offered to climb in with the prisoner to guard him and likely get some credit for his capture, Longarm agreed that seemed a fine idea. He was no fool. So, in the end, the whole affair only resulted in him getting to work twenty-odd minutes later than usual. Longarm hadn't made it to the office on time for a coon's age.

As he entered the front office on the second story of the Denver Federal Building a few blocks from the shoot-out, young Henry, the pallid-faced priss who acted as Billy Vail's clerk and kept casual visitors from pestering the boss in the back, shot Longarm a now-you're-gonna-get-it! smirk. So Longarm didn't have to ask if U.S. Marshal William Vail was in a good mood or not this morning. He just strode on back to the oak-paneled office and sat down across the desk from old Billy Vail to take his chewing like a man.

4

Billy Vail chewed good. He figured he had to. He was a tough old lawman who didn't look tough and knew he didn't look tough. The erstwhile Texas Ranger had gone to lard riding herd on his more active deputies behind a desk, and he had one of those smooth round faces that made a man look like a sort of bushy-browed baby instead of a man of destiny as he got ever older. So while one or two mule skinners and Calamity Jane could at least match old Billy Vail in a cussing contest, when he wasn't really sore, Longarm was braced for some pungent comments indeed as his boss shot a weary glance at the banjo clock on the wall and took a deep breath. But then Henry came in to tell them reporters from the *News* and *Post* were outside, wanting to interview someone about the capture of Amarillo Jack.

Vail shot Henry a sincerely puzzled frown, scowled at Longarm, and demanded, "What in thunder's going on here?"

So Longarm got out a three-for-a-nickel cheroot as he explained, "Not here. Over by Fourteenth and Larimer. I shot it out with Amarillo Jack on my way to work, and guess who won."

He felt it might be safe now to light up in Billy Vail's office. So he thumbed a kitchen match aflame and proceeded to do so as his boss favored him with a fatherly smile and muttered, "All right, forget what I was just about to say about your habit of molesting snails on your way to work. How did you ever manage to get here before noon after gunning a want in such a sissified town? Doesn't the coroner want depositions in triplicate anymore?"

Longarm took a drag on his cheroot, exhaled, and replied, "I took him alive. I'd have brung him

5

along with me if he'd been able to walk. But right now he can't even hobble. I busted his leg as we were disputing my plans for this weekend. If County General knows its trade he ought to be outa a hip cast in, oh, six to eight weeks. Thighbones heal faster than shinbones as a rule."

Vail whistled in admiration and said, "You done right for a change, old son. That mad-dog son of a bitch is wanted hither and yon for so many killings it's a good thing they can only hang a man once. The expenses on the ropes alone would be awesome if they had to dangle him for *all* the dirt he's done." Vail opened a desk drawer and fumbled out a sheaf of Wanted fliers as he added, "I swear, I don't know who to wire first. At a nickel a word this office will be stuck three figures if we bother with each and every court throughout this and other lands as want to hang the son of a bitch. He murdered a mounty up Canada way a year or so back, and just last winter he back-shot a couple of Mex rurales in Ciudad Juarez."

Longarm raised an eyebrow at him. So Billy sighed and explained, "I feel the same way about the rurales as a general rule. But on that occasion Amarillo Jack sort of overdid it, even for a Texas boy. He was in a Juarez cantina set aside for Yanqui tourists to drink in peace. Nobody was pestering him. The two Mex lawmen were at the bar with their backs to him and didn't even know he was there when he simply butchered 'em both from behind."

Longarm grimaced and said, "It's generally agreed the cuss was born bad and grew up worse, Billy. You're the boss. But if I were you and had to pick, I'd just send him over to Fort Smith as soon as he's fit for transporting. You know how sentimental some courts are about homicidal lunatics, and Judge Isaac Parker says insanity pleas don't cut no ice with him."

Vail shrugged and muttered, "Maybe not when old Isaac first got started on cleaning things up in the Indian Nation. Lately the newspaper sob sisters have been rawhiding him about his old-fashioned notions of right and wrong. I've heard that of late the court at Fort Smith has been entertaining appeals and even granting stays of execution on old boys with slick-talking lawyers. Amarillo Jack hails from a big and prosperous Texas cattle clan. They could no doubt manage a team of lawyers for their black sheep if they wanted to, and you just can't get around the simple fact that he has to be mad as a hatter, you know."

Longarm just blew a thoughtful smoke ring. It wasn't his worry. Henry asked what about those newspapermen out front and Longarm said, "Tell 'em I'm off hunting the James-Younger gang, and if that don't get rid of 'em, I can always duck out the side door."

Henry went on looking uncertain. Vail nodded and said, "The less publicity this office gets, the fewer answers Washington is likely to pester me for. We don't have to worry about sending the rascal anywhere before he's fit to travel. So I mean to just sit tight for now and see who hollers loudest for him."

The pudgy Vail glanced back at Longarm and added, "I like your notion about slipping out the other way. You'd have had the afternoon off in any case. Meanwhile, I'll invite the pests back here and spoon-feed 'em the old banana oil. If we just announce that, sure, we got Amarillo Jack on ice, period, the papers will let the rest of the world know we're holding him, and anyone who wants him bad enough can pay Western Union a nickel a damned word. So what are you waiting for, Longarm, a kiss good-bye?"

Longarm told his boss not to talk so fresh and by the time the newspapermen had been led back to Vail's office by Henry, Longarm was on his way down the marble steps to the street. It was still a mite early to show up, but he expected the widow woman who was expecting him wouldn't mind. She'd been stuck with entertaining relations from back East at her brownstone mansion up on Sherman Avenue, and she kissed a heap better than Billy Vail might, even when she wasn't hard-up and horny as she'd allowed she was in that perfumed note she'd sent to him that morning. So Henry had to run like hell to catch up with Longarm on the corner of Colfax and Broadway, gasping for breath and cussing a lot more manly than he looked. As Longarm stopped and turned to Henry with a quizzical smile, the breathless clerk gasped, "He told me I'd find you headed up to Sherman Avenue. He said to make sure you got to work by dawn, no later, come Monday morning. You'll be relieving Deputy Guilfoyle at the Rex Hotel. Marshal Vail has to send a man up to Broomfield to look into a fence war and Guilfoyle's the best field man free."

Longarm looked modestly injured as he asked, "Since when and how come? I'm senior to Guilfoyle and I know the country up near Broomfield better than most, since I investigated that post office robbery up there just a spell back."

Henry wheezed, "Look, I just work here. Marshal Vail says he means to send Guilfoyle because anyone he sends might get tied up a spell around Broomfield. He wants you to change places, guarding a federal witness at the hotel because the timing works out better. The witness will have finished giving testimony here in Denver just about the time that Amarillo Jack figures to be getting about on crutches and leg irons. So guess who gets to transport him?"

Longarm swore softly and said, "If it wasn't for those reporters cluttering up the office right now I'd go back and fuss at the old fool personal! I'm a senior deputy, and where in the rule book does it say I get stuck with such beginner's chores? Amarillo Jack in a hip cast as well as irons could be transported by any armed and dangerous woman or, hell, even *you*, no offense!"

Henry sniffed and said, "Gee, thanks. I don't think Marshal Vail is worried about the prisoner escaping on the way as much as he is the ceremony involved in turning him over to the Mexican authorities. You do speak Spanish and—"

"Hold on!" Longarm cut in, staring down at Henry in growing dismay as he demanded, "Who said anything about turning that lunatic over to the crazy *rurales* of all folk?"

"It came up just now as the boss was talking with Crawford of the *Post*. You know El Presidente Diaz has the habit of saying, with some justification, that the U.S. Justice Department refuses to cooperate with Mexican courts."

Longarm snorted in disgust and replied, "We don't cooperate with kangaroos, worth mention, for the same reasons." Then he considered and decided, "All right. I can see the method in old Billy's

9

madness. Throwing a mad dog to the mad dogs running poor old Mexico right now makes a certain sense when you study on it. Somebody has to hang Amarillo Jack, and enjoying the pleasure of it all might calm the growls south of the border just a mite. But Billy can't have *me* in mind as the transporting officer, Henry. It's a simple fact of nature that Mexico has more than one death warrant posted on me, personal, for gunning rurales in maybe a more seemly manner than the bone Billy wants to throw to 'em!"

Henry shrugged and said, "I just type up travel orders the way Marshal Vail orders me to. I could be wrong. But unless I am, I expect you'll be on your way to Juarez by the end of the month."

Henry had to be wrong. Even the widow woman up on Sherman Avenue could see that, once Longarm got around to telling her that a week or so of nights, with him guarding an infernal witness by day, was all they had to look forward to.

By the time they'd gotten around to such idle conversation, of course, they'd spent some time in her big four-poster with the bottle of champagne she'd been keeping on ice all the previous week. She said his mustache tickled her nose as well but just moaned "Ooh!" or "Ahh!" to other parts of him he did his best to tickle her with. Since they were old pals, used to each other's bare bodies in broad day, they found it easy and sort of nice to converse about this and that as they went on fornicating in a calmer manner, once they'd recovered from the first excitement. So she was kneeling across the bed, smoothing her long light brown hair on the white linen her cheek was pressed to as

10

Longarm stood barefoot on the rug, thrusting in and out of the ample charms she'd raised up to receive any further bounty he might have to offer. The view from where he was standing was a mite inspiring for shop talk. But he'd been raised to answer his elders politely when they spoke to him and so, since she was a year or more older than him and had just tried to get him to quit his job, again, he gripped her hipbones reassuringly, thrust in as deep as he could get, and said, "I can't give up such a swell job just because my boss has gone senile on me, honey lamb. I've already put in six or eight years with the Justice Department, and even if I knew of a cattle outfit that retired a man on half-pay, for life, I'd have never switched from herding cows to chasing owlhoots if I'd admired cows that much."

She arched her spine to murmur, "Ooh, nice. Don't stop and don't you even think about going down Mexico way before Mexico gets a new and hopefully more sensible government! I thought Marshal Vail had issued standing orders for you to stay at least a full ten miles north or south of either border, dear."

He sort of rotated it inside her, causing her to gasp with added pleasure, as he explained, "It wasn't my fault. On the rare occasions I've had to chase wants into Mexico or Canada, I've done my best to act neighborly. Is it my fault lawmen both to the north and south don't share my views on simple justice? The rurales wouldn't savvy justice if they could read and write, while those picky Canadian mounties seem to whip out a rule book every two minutes, just to pester me about laws I never heard of. I reckon that's only to be expected in a country where the judges put on white wigs as makes 'em look like bird dogs and, ah, could we talk about it some more, later?"

She wanted to finish old-fashioned, too, albeit she somehow wound up on top before they had. Then she got up as if she was used to wandering all over the house without a stitch on in broad day, and by the time she was back with another bottle of iced champagne he had his breath back. So she forked a shapely bare thigh across his and uncorked the bottle in a sassy position indeed, even if what she was kissing with her gaping love lips was just pressed between them, half limp if not all the way wrung out.

She had to wriggle about on him some more to get the tumblers from the night table near the bed and refill them. She spilled some cold bubbly on both of them and giggled. It tickled him as well. He offered to lick her clean. But she said the sun was still up, for land's sake, and since they had a whole night for "that sort of thing," whatever she meant by that, she wanted to talk "seriously," which always meant a man was in trouble if he didn't pay mighty close attention.

So he clinked glasses with her and listened sharp as she told him, "That silly clerk could have been just confused. But what are we to do if Marshal Vail really wants to send you to Mexico with that outlaw you captured, darling?"

Longarm swallowed some bubbly and told her, "*We* don't have to do nothing. He frowns on my taking gals along with me in the field. I reckon I'll just have to go, by myself."

She insisted, "You *can't* go to Mexico, you sweet fool. I won't let you. Juarez is a dangerous place for any Anglo to visit right now and— What's that story

I've heard about you invading Mexico that time with a shapely Texas tomboy and an Oriental hired gun to take on the whole Mexican army, with field artillery, for land's sake?"

He smiled up at her—it wasn't easy—and told her, "It was a story, like you just said. Neither me nor James Butler Hickok ever got this friendly with Calamity Jane, neither, no matter what she tells newspaper reporters."

The much prettier and probably younger widow woman he *was* in bed with sipped some bubbly to peer archly down at him over the rim of her glass to observe, "I'll take your word on Calamity Jane. I've seen pictures of her. As to that blonde you invaded Mexico with that time . . . Well, I wasn't there, which may have been just as well for both of you. My point is that whatever you did down there, the Mexican government has put a price on both your heads. I read that in the *Denver Post*. Doesn't your crazy old boss even read the *local* papers?"

He saw she was too distracted to refill their glasses. So he took the bottle from her to pour as he replied, "Old Billy ain't crazy. You and Henry, between you, must be making a mountain out of a molehill. I'll ask Billy what he really said when I have to report to him, come Monday morning. Unless, of course, you'd like me to ask him sooner. Him and his wife live just down the avenue a ways, and he ought to be getting home for supper any time now. So if you want to roll off and let me get at my boots . . ."

She must not have wanted him to. She got rid of both the bottle and their glasses to reach down between them and see if she could somehow get it in her again despite its present lack of inspiration. He

13

sighed and said, "You're doing just fine. But I wish you'd make up your mind, sweet fingers. Are we talking about my going or coming, right now?"

She assured him verbally and manually of her desires of the moment and it was sure fun, letting it rise slowly to the occasion amid such inspiring surroundings. But, later, sated for the moment but still sprawled atop him with her thighs still hugging him and her soft long hair spread to dry on his bare chest, she had to break the spell by murmuring, as she nibbled his collarbone, "You don't really have to go anywhere, Monday morning, you know. My standing offer is still good and you told me, last time, that you'd think about it."

He didn't answer. She waited a few moments. Then she sighed and said, "Men. I just don't understand the way your brain could be so different when all the other parts of you seem to fit mine so nice, Custis. It's not as if I ever asked you to marry up with me, all the way, damnit. Why can't you just sort of stay here with me all the time and just forget that silly job before it gets you killed? I know what they pay you for risking your life, Custis. Would it surprise you to learn I spend that much a year on cosmetics and perfume?"

He patted her bare rump tenderly and told her, "Nope. I was aware of how swell you smelled the first night I carried you up here. What would we tell your neighbors if I took you up on your offer? That I was your gardener or, seeing I ain't so skilled at clipping hedges, just a sort of orphan child you'd brung home to raise?"

She bit down harder on his collarbone and insisted, "Don't try to make it sound sordid, damnit. If I cared what the damned neighbors thought we

14

wouldn't be having this silly conversation. Half the women in town seem to know I'm just the poor silly widow woman you use as a mere play-pretty." She laughed, bitterly, and added, "I think some of them must be jealous. Why don't we just go all the way and shock them good by, well, shacking up and to hell with my reputation, or the thought of losing you? Lord knows we don't need the pittance the government pays you, darling. I have plenty of money, and if you'd feel better about it if I were to simply transfer some to your own bank account—"

"Don't talk dirty," he warned her with an edge to his voice that told her he meant it. He held her closer, but said, "My job ain't silly, to me. It's a job that has to be done. I know the pay ain't much, and to tell the pure truth, I'd rather be here in the arms of such a beautiful woman than many a place Billy Vail has sent me in the past and figures to send me again. It ain't true that I enjoy hunting men down, and sometimes when I catch up with one that isn't all bad I just hate to do what I sometimes have to do. But I do what I'm supposed to do, and when I've done things right, it makes me feel . . . right."

"Like some sort of knight in shining armor?" she asked with just a hint of mockery.

So he thought about that before he told her, "I met an outlaw dressed in armor one time. Never tried it myself. Try her this way. One time I saved a lady, a dumb and ugly lady, and her kids, from a gang of crooks. I saved their hardscrabble spread and the little money they had, as well. She never thanked me. She was bawling too hard as I rode away. But as I rode, I suspected I knew just how old Saint George felt about that dragon. I've yet to meet a dragon, riding for Billy Vail, but there's a

15

heap of mortal pests out there and somebody, call him a fool if you like, has to *do* something about 'em. So let's say no more about Monday morning and I'll be proud to show you as swell a weekend as the two of us can likely stand."

So, being a smart as well as lusty old gal, she shut up about the future, and by Monday she'd been loved too silly to fix him a proper breakfast. So he reported for work hungry as well as walking kind of funny.

Chapter 2

The Rex was one of Denver's newer and more modernized hotels. So they had gaslight, steam heat and indoor plumbing on every floor. Better yet, they had an all-night dining room just off the lobby, and the night man, Smiley, was a good sport about letting Longarm grub down some chili con carne and apple pie with two cups of coffee before taking over the guard detail. As they shook on it in the lobby Longarm asked Smiley if there were any special instructions as went with the chore. The saturnine Smiley, who never seemed to smile, despite his last name, said, "I ain't even seen her, so far. A couple of old boys from the prosecutor's office come to fetch her to court and back between sunrise and sunset, according to old Guilfoyle. She's in a private suite with her own bath on the third floor. Door's locked and barred on the inside, of course. You go

17

up now and again to make sure nobody's knocked it off its hinges. If she needs you for anything she has orders to call down on the house telephone and never to open her door to anyone, see?"

Longarm nodded and observed, "They must be worried about her. What sort of a case is it and who might be out to shut her up?"

Smiley shrugged and said, "Can't say. I've yet to see the fool gal and nobody's come calling on her after dark whilst I've been posted here. It ain't so bad earlier in the evening. But I sure get tired of staring at spittoons and rubber plants in the wee small hours. Guilfoyle could likely tell you more, if Billy left him on the day watch instead of you. What's the story on that case they sent Guilfoyle on?"

Longarm hauled out a cheroot as he muttered, "Old Billy never tells me much, either. I didn't even know the witness upstairs was a female until just now. You go on home to that Arapaho gal you're so fond of, and farther along, like the old song says, somebody may tell me more about it. What's the room number, just in case someone suspicious comes in here asking?"

Smiley said, "Room thirty-three. Nobody but us is supposed to know which room she's in. So feel free to be suspicious as you like and, by the way, I ain't shacked up with that Arapaho gal no more. She gets too romantical after dark to stay true to a poor old boy Billy Vail keeps sticking with night duty. I got me a night-sleeping barmaid, now. She may not be much to look at, but I ain't caught her in bed with nobody but me yet."

Longarm agreed most women were as wicked as men when it came to such matters. So Smiley left and Longarm sat down in a leather chair shaded by a corner rubber plant and lit his smoke, knowing he was in for a mighty long day. They'd never told him about this sort of duty when he'd signed up as a federal deputy. He'd been under the impression he'd never have to pull guard duty again when he'd gotten out of the infernal army.

Longarm seldom jawed about his army days. Bitter memories of the war were still fresh and it wasn't always clear whether a gent you were drinking with had fought for the Blue or the Grey. But if there was one thing vets of either side agreed on, it was that, next to being pinned down under artillery fire, nothing was more disgusting than pulling Kitchen Police or Interior Guard.

Which was worse depended on which shit detail one was stuck with at the moment. One tended to pine for guard duty whilst scrubbing pots and pans with lye soap for the same reasons one felt sure peeling spuds and swapping jokes in a noisy kitchen tent had to feel less tedious than just staring into space on guard, waiting for something—*anything*, for Pete's sake—to damnit *happen*!

Nine hundred and ninety-nine times out of a thousand, nothing did. So that added to the torture if you were at all bright. It was that one time in a thousand you had to watch for, knowing how much trouble you could get into if you missed it, even as you felt almost dead certain that nothing was going to happen. Longarm took his duties serious and knew Billy Vail knew he did. That only served to make him hate this chore even more than less-attentive lawmen. Deputy Bell, down New Mexico way, had no doubt stood guard many a tedious time before that fatal split second his mind wandered and Billy the Kid jumped him in the Lincoln County Jail.

Longarm had a clear view of the hotel desk and only had to crank his neck a mite to cover the front entrance from his comfortable corner seat. Lest he get too comfortable, he made a point of standing up each time he lit a fresh smoke, and he made himself wait a full five minutes between light-ups because he knew a man chain-smoking sort of forgot he was smoking, and any craving, however slight, tended to keep a man aware of his surroundings. Things brightened up for a spell as hotel guests started coming down the stairwell to check out or go to work. Longarm managed to crave at least a few of the better looking ones, albeit mildly, thanks to that glorious weekend up on Sherman Avenue. He was sort of sorry he wasn't really hard-up. He only got to see most of the no doubt honest working gals from the rear, and they'd all left for work before eight in any case. Nobody came to check in. That allowed him to ponder railroad timetables in his head for a spell. But it didn't take long. For like any lawman worth his salt, Longarm already knew the times trains would be rolling in and out of town, and nobody would be getting off this side of noon, now.

He was on his feet, lighting yet another smoke, when Billy Vail came in as if he thought he was some infernal corporal of the guard. Longarm resisted an impulse to leap out from behind a lobby pillar and yell "Boo!" Old Billy was quick on the draw as well as devoid of a sense of fun. So Longarm just saluted and yelled, "Nothing to report on or near this post, sir!"

Vail winced, favored Longarm with a disgusted

look, and took the seat his deputy had just climbed out of before he muttered, "This chicken shit wasn't my grand notion. When the federal court down the hall from me orders a witness guarded I don't have much to say about it. I ain't here checking up on you. I stopped by County General on my way to the office this morning. Amarillo Jack is hanging tough and refused to even tell me what time it was. But, thanks to the lead you put in him they had to drug him silly before they could probe the wound and set his leg bone."

Vail got out one of his awful cigars, as if in self-defense, and bit the tip off to spit it into a nearby spittoon with considerable skill before he added, "Nursing sisters talk more than mad-dog killers, if you approach 'em polite." Then he lit his cigar, leaned back expansively, and smiled up at Longarm to say, "He was hired to do you, old son. Amarillo Jack has been known to back-shoot just for practice, as we already knew. But it seems that on this occasion his gun hand was being rented by the hour. In morphine-induced chagrin he confided to a pretty nurse that as soon as he finished killing you he'd have a thousand silver cartwheels to spend on her."

Longarm blew a thoughtful smoke ring and decided, "That's sort of flattering. Many a man's been back-shot for less. Was the gal smart enough to get any names out of the groggy rascal?"

Vail shook his head to reply in a disgusted tone, "The fool woman put more dope in him to knock him out entire. When I called her an idiot she wept bitter tears and evoked the name of some Greek hypocrite. Then a stuffy sawbones fussed at me as well. They're confused as hell at County General.

21

They seem to think saving the son of a bitch's leg is more important than getting the truth out of him. A couple of Denver copper-badges are posted nearby to keep him in bed for us until he's fit to be moved. But when I asked the docs to shoot some more dope in Amarillo Jack they acted like I'd suggested abusing him. We're going to have to get it out of him ourselves once he's turned over to us for transporting."

Longarm frowned thoughtfully and decided, "That could be sort of a poker game, even if we poke him some. With his wits about him he'd be as likely to name an enemy as the friend who hired him, you know."

"Mad dogs don't have many friends. He let it slip to that gal it was a purely cash transaction. Your best bet would be a better offer, on your way to Juarez, where you could say I neither knew nor approved, see?"

Longarm took a long thoughtful drag on his cheroot and let all the smoke trickle out his nostrils before he replied, "Henry told me you'd said something about having me deliver the murderous rascal to the rurales. I thought, at the time, Henry had to be a mite confused. What was that you said, that time, about having my ass as well as my badge if I ever went anywhere near Ciudad Juarez again?"

Billy Vail chuckled fondly at the memory and said, "Well, you did cause an international incident the last time you enjoyed some cactus candy down yonder. But that Mex death warrant on old Amarillo Jack might just offer us the chance to mend some fences. You know we hardly ever turn even a disgusting gringo over to the rough justice of El Presidente Diaz. So Mexico ought to be mighty

22

pleased at our sudden and unusual cooperation. It ain't often they get to execute a Yanqui with Uncle Sam's blessings."

Longarm objected, "They get to execute *two* of us at once even less often. Have you forgotten they have me on their shit list as well?"

Billy Vail nodded, but said, "That's what I mean by mending fences. I've been on the wire to Mexico City over the weekend. The U.S. State Department chimed in toward the last as we were fussing over the final details. I'd be just a big fibber if I said the rurales wanted you to marry even one of their sisters. But they want Amarillo Jack so bad they're willing to overlook past misunderstandings they've had with you, as long as you're willing to just turn your prisoner over to 'em and not shoot any more of 'em."

Longarm grimaced and insisted, "I'd trust Amarillo Jack as far as I'd trust that oily Diaz. What's to stop them from double-crossing us? Diaz only got to be El Presidente by double-crossing his own political party when poor old Juarez died. Be it recorded that Benito Juarez left Mexico with a constitution modeled on our own, which Diaz tore up before the funeral was over. How can even our State Department hold Mexico to its word when it's being run by a gang of thugs that make the James-Younger gang resemble Puritans?"

Vail hid his pudgy face behind an octopus cloud of cigar smoke as he replied soothingly, "I know the rurales are no damned good. So does Amarillo Jack. That's the sneaky *second* string of our bow. He'll be on his way to a no doubt painfully protracted execution with a lawman known by friend and foe alike to be a man of his word. It's a long

23

train ride. He'll have plenty of time to consider the error of his ways as every clicky-clack carries him closer to the tender mercies of Mex lawmen who just hate him like hell. I'd let *him* suggest a deal, first, if I was you."

Longarm shrugged and said, "That sounds reasonable, since I don't have any deal in mind, save for turning him over sudden on the bridge and ducking for cover even faster."

Vail nodded sagely and said, "You might see fit to admit you'd as soon run him over to Fort Smith, where the hangings are handled more scientific, provided, of course, he was willing to make it worth your extra time and the scolding you'd likely get from me."

Longarm brightened, started to ask an obvious question, then nodded and said, "I like it. I want to take him to Juarez about as much as I want to jump off a cliff with him. But since he won't be reading my mind, he might just be willing to tell me who hired him to kill me, in exchange for a few more days of life and a much more comfortable death. I'll tell him how old George Maledon takes professional pride in his hanging chores over to Fort Smith. They say he uses rope-length tables worked out over in London by English experts on the subject, so as to neither drop a man so far as to tear off the head or choke him to death slow by not dropping him far enough. I'll assure him old George will weigh him and measure his neck just before his rope dance, to make sure it all goes well."

Vail grimaced and said, "I wouldn't overdo the details if I were you. Just hint that you're more interested in who hired him to kill you than you might be about who gets to kill him. He ought to come clean by the time you reach Santa Fe."

Longarm nodded and said, "Right. That's a good place to transfer to the eastbound for Fort Smith."

But Vail shook his head and said, "I don't want you to take him to Fort Smith. He's been promised to the Mex authorities down in Juarez. So that's where I want him delivered."

Longarm blinked in disbelief and demanded, "Are you asking me to make a promise and go back on it, Billy?"

"I ain't asking. I'm ordering. Where in the U.S. Constitution does it say word-one about us having to deal straight with hired killers?"

So Longarm gripped his cheroot with bared teeth to reach for his wallet, unpin his federal badge from the same, and flatly state, "I reckon I answer to a more fussy code. I've been known to lie with a gun trained on my head. But I just don't *take* orders like that last one, Billy."

He dropped his badge in his superior's lap as he added with weary resignation, "I just turned down a position as a sort of hired stud. I thought at the time it might make me feel like an infernal pimp. But I see there are lower positions than pimping, after all, and guarding this lobby was a pain in the ass to start with."

Vail sighed and said, "Oh, shit, I'll send one of the other boys to Juarez with Amarillo Jack and you can just go on guessing who hired him to back-shoot you. It's your own fool back you're being so honorable about." Then he rose wearily to his feet, handed the badge back to Longarm, and said, "You ain't allowed to quit whilst you're on guard duty, and Deputy Flynn won't be here to relieve you before suppertime. Are we straight, now, you poor misguided man of your word?"

Longarm grinned, said he'd think about it, and pinned the badge back in his wallet while Billy Vail grumped out to head on to the office, muttering to himself.

Longarm consulted his pocket watch and sat down again. The argument with his boss had killed some time, but not nearly enough. Things got tedious as hell again. Then he had to take a leak. So he went over to the desk, asked the old gent herding keys and mail where the facilities might be, and when told the way to the lobby leakery, Longarm asked what time those gents from the federal court usually came to pick up the mystery guest in room 33. The clerk glanced at a nearby wall clock and said, "Nine, sharp, as a rule. That gives you ten or more minutes to shake the dew from your lilly if you want to talk to them."

Longarm knew he didn't have that much water backed up in him. So he took the time to ask if the clerk knew just who the gal in 33 was, and what she might be doing up there so much.

The clerk shrugged and said, "Well, nobody's supposed to even know which room she's in. But a man has eyes and ears. I hear tell the government is trying some big-shot contractor for defrauding the Bureau of Indian Affairs. Miss Aurora Stone, up in thirty-three, was the gent's bookkeeper whilst he was billing Uncle Sam for flour that was mostly bran, and corned beef as was really dog food. They say it was her as turned her boss in and nobody knows half as much as she might about his crookery. It's her own notion that her boss might be out to silence her for good, however. If you ask me, a man on trial would have to be a total fool to have a witness murdered while the jury was still pondering his fate."

Longarm hadn't asked the old gent's opinion. So he saw no need to tell him he was full of it and simply headed for the back to empty his own bladder. The gent's room was clean and up to date as the rest of the Rex, as far as he could see in the dark. They'd trimmed the wall fixtures to save on gas during the slow hours of the hotel business. But he'd pissed in the dark before and even got to wash his hands, afterwards, and dry them on a roll towel that hadn't been used much. Then he heard a shotgun go off, twice, out front, and tore out of the gent's room with his own gun ready for anything. But all he saw in the otherwise empty lobby was an already thinning haze of gunsmoke.

He called out to the clerk, who gingerly raised his head from behind the marble countertop to ask, "What happened?"

Longarm didn't know either. So he strode to the front entrance, and while the crowded street out front looked normal, he spotted a ten-gauge shotgun shell on the white tiles of the vestibule and hunkered down to pick it up before going back inside. He showed it to the clerk, saying, "This is a live round of number-nine buck. Somebody dropped it as they fumbled to load just in off the street. Then he, she, or it, fired the barrels they *did* manage to load, here in the lobby. Your turn."

The clerk said, "I ducked when that horrendous double blast went off right in my ear! I didn't take time to stare about as I hit the floor. I got good at ducking at a place called Cold Harbor. That's how come I'm still alive."

27

Longarm didn't ask which side he'd been on. He said, "If the scatter gun had been aimed at you, ducking after you heard it go off wouldn't have worked. So they had to be shooting at somebody else, right?"

The clerk grimaced and replied, "That only works to a point. With you in the gent's room, the lobby was empty." Then he gasped and added, "Oh, shit!" So Longarm gazed the same way and said the same thing as they both regarded the leather chair he'd been seated in most of the morning. Two charges of number-nine buck had sure played hell with the upholstery. Horsehair stuffing had even wound up hanging like Spanish moss from the nearby rubber plants and the floor could use a good sweeping, now, as well. As the clerk was still protesting such vandalism a brace of gents dressed like lawyers with guns bulging under their frock coats came in, sniffing curiously at the reek of gunsmoke.

It saved some tedious questions when both recognized Longarm and he recalled one of them from earlier court duties. The one he knew said, "Morning, Longarm. How come you just shot up that chair with that pistol you seem to be pointing at me?"

Longarm lowered his .44-40 to a politer angle as he replied, "We were just talking about that. It wasn't me. I'd say a sort of nervous type stepped in off the street, fumbled some shells into a double-barrel sawed-off he'd been toting under, say, a long coat, and just blasted where I was supposed to be sitting without taking the time to make sure I was really there. Now you know as much about it as we do."

The two men from the prosecutor's office exchanged glances, then they were running up the stairs as fast as they could manage, their own guns out.

The clerk gasped, "What on earth?"

So Longarm explained, "They want to make sure their witness is all right. I could have told them nobody got by me. But what the hell, they'd likely come to fetch her in any case."

They had. A few minutes later the two of them came back down, a lot slower, with a pale and shaken but sort of pretty little brunette between them. They didn't offer to introduce Longarm to her. But he ticked his hat brim to her, anyway, and as they were hauling her out the front door, called after them, "Hey, what time are you boys likely to bring Miss Aurora back here?"

The one he knew called back that the trial was winding down and not to bank on any particular time. Then they were out of sight and Longarm was free to tell the clerk, "I just hate this sort of duty. Don't you?"

The clerk had recovered enough to smile thinly and reply, "It sure is hell on the furniture. But if that trial is about over, won't that mean your federal gents won't have to worry about the safety of that little witness gal?"

Longarm shrugged and answered, *"Quien sabe?* I know less than you seem to about the case. A trial ain't over until it's over, and that includes appeals when you're a big shot with a stable of slick lawyers. I've a mind to drift on over to the Federal Building and watch, since there's no way anyone can murder the little gal in this hotel, right now. But they whipped out of here too fast for me to suggest that and my own boss can be such a fuss. Might there be a saloon in this part of town where a man can keep one eye on yonder front door, just in case?"

The clerk wistfully suggested the Golden Eagle, catty-corner across the street, and asked just who might want to pay the Rex for a new lobby chair.

It was a good question. Longarm considered and decided, "I'd say the Denver District Court, federal, owed you at least an upholstery job, seeing I was guarding one of their witnesses when somebody tried to get through me." Then he started to say something else but didn't. There was no sense sticking his own office for the bill, even if it did seem just as likely the attack had been meant more personal. Amarillo Jack had more or less confessed he'd been sent to back-shoot a well-known lawman, not a bitty bookkeeper. So it was just as likely that, having failed with Amarillo Jack, the mysterious son of a bitch who was after him had simply sent in a member of his scrub team. By now the rascal was no doubt mighty vexed. Longarm knew that *he* was.

Chapter 3

Longarm never drank enough on duty to cloud his mind, and didn't much like getting drunk at any time. He simply enjoyed the taste of cold needled beer and was big enough to absorb a few schooners of the same without feeling the effects a more sissy-built gent might have.

But while the beer on tap in the Golden Eagle was fine and the free lunch was grand, albeit a mite salty, Longarm's heart just wasn't in it as he leaned against the mahogany near the front window. He'd have felt a heap more comfortable with his back to a wall. But he couldn't sit forted up in a corner and watch the hotel entrance across the way at the same time. It had been dumb of Billy Vail to detail a deputy in such an uncertain position to guard a witness. For as soon as one studied on the matter, it seemed obvious that the

31

gunslick or more after him figured to put the gal in added jeopardy. That poor old room clerk had come close to having his head blown off and nobody at all could be after *him*! So Longarm aimed to ask Vail to take him off this fool detail the moment he had the chance. It was a heap easier to catch someone gunning for you when you knew for sure who he was gunning for. As things now stood, the nervous nelly with the ten gauge could have been after *either* of 'em, and the poor little bookkeeper had enough to worry about without getting caught in cross-fire that had nothing to do with her appearances in court. The clerk had a point when he'd mentioned the foolishness of gunning a witness in a simple fraud case. No matter what she proved her employer had been up to, it seemed unlikely he'd catch more than five-at-hard with time off for good behavior. If he had her murdered, as the prime and obvious suspect, he could wind up staring up a rope and dancing in the wind, and anyone slick enough to defraud the government likely knew that.

He finished his first schooner and shook his head politely when the barkeep asked if he'd like another. He said, "Your suds are fine. But I'm feeling more proddy than thirsty right now. So I'll just stretch my fool legs some more whilst I have the time."

He ambled back across the street to the hotel. Inside, he found the shot-up chair had been hauled off somewhere, and they hadn't replaced it with another. He approached the desk to ask the same clerk for the key to Room 33. The clerk shook his head and said, "Ain't got it. One of them lawmen from the courthouse has it. They let her in and out and keep it between visits."

Longarm frowned thoughtfully and asked, "Do tell? How does Miss Aurora get in and out of her room when they ain't here?"

The clerk explained her door unlocked from the inside with a latch, in case of, say, a hotel fire, and that the gal hadn't seen fit to go in and out on her own since she'd been staying at the Rex on Uncle Sam. He added, "She calls down on the telly-phone for room service if she needs anything, and lets the help in. Otherwise, not even the chambermaids can get in when she ain't there. We told 'em we could vouch for all our hired help, but you know how fussy some folk are."

Longarm nodded, ambled over to another lobby chair and hauled it into the corner he'd been seated in before. When the clerk shot him a reproachful look he said, "I ain't about to *stand* in a corner until suppertime, and this is the best spot to cover the front door and stairwell from."

But he'd barely lit up and sat down before he had a better idea and, seeing the lobby was as empty as it ever got, went up the stairs himself. Climbing to the third story did a lot to get his legs less wobbly after so little rest up to Sherman Avenue over the weekend and so little exercise since.

Room 33 was easy enough to find. He got out his innocent-looking pocketknife and opened a blade that could have resulted in his arrest if he hadn't been packing his own badge. The cunningly notched blade made short work of the fairly standard hotel lock. He stepped inside for a look-see and wasn't too surprised when there was nothing unexpected to see. All the room furnishings were the property of the Rex, purchased by an interior decorator without much imagination. The framed prints on the walls clashed loudly with the orange flowers of the wallpaper, and Longarm could have told them purple drapes and bed covers just didn't go with orange wallpaper and a green rug. A lady's overnight bag stood open atop a chest of drawers. There was a more substantial suitcase in the wardrobe closet, along with a dainty nightgown and some bed slippers. The gal had spread some toilet articles on the dressing table. The perfumed soap in the adjoining bath was likely her own private stock as well. Near the bed, some women's magazines and a romance novel lay beside the ticking brass alarm clock she'd no doubt taken from her overnight bag as well. It was the sort of clock a bookkeeper who liked to get to work on time would have had. So how come it was reading seven-thirty when it was closer to noon everywhere else?

He decided it was natural enough to forget to wind an alarm clock when gents came to carry you to court so late in the day. He turned to leave. Then he turned to stare back at that clock some more. He picked it up and held it to his ear. He'd been right about it being run down. It wasn't ticking at all. So what in thunder *was*?

It didn't take Longarm long to find the infernal device, once he'd decided there might be one, somewhere in the lady's room. It was under her bedsprings, wired in place against the middle of her bed. It consisted of four sticks of dynamite, studded with carpet tacks, connected to a dry cell and another alarm clock set to ring, mighty loud, at midnight, when even a restless young gal would at least be reading in bed.

As he gingerly disconnected the crude but deadly device Longarm muttered, "All right, you couldn't have been meant for *me*. I don't know the witness that well and get off at suppertime in any case."

Then he set the dismembered bomb on the bed table and told it, "If you'd been planted before noon you'd have gone off by this time. It's barely after noon, right now. So I just missed meeting someone sneaky in the hall outside." He picked up the dynamite and left the more harmless parts where they were, for now, as he let himself out and went back downstairs.

He didn't show the tack-studded dynamite to the room clerk. He didn't even say where he'd just been. He said, "Someone who works here, or stays here during daylight hours, has been pussy-footing, unless you can recall someone checking in or out within the last hour or so."

The clerk looked blank and said, "You're the only one who's passed by this desk since those other gents left with that witness gal. What sort of pussy-footing are we talking about?"

"I'm still working on that. Might there be a back or side door to this hotel, pard?"

The clerk nodded and said, "Sure. There's a service entrance facing the back alley and there's a fire door as well, over behind them Boston ferns by yonder writing desk. Why do you ask?"

Longarm swore under his breath and said, "*Now* they tell me. I like the back door best. Any sneak with a shotgun who knew about that side door would have used it this morning."

The clerk protested, "Nobody who wasn't employed by this hotel could use either. They're both locked from inside, see?"

Longarm grimaced and said, "I could tell you things about locked doors, but I don't want to lead a lad your age into temptation. In sum, almost any son of a bitch could have snuck in or out just now. Don't you just love a limited list of possible suspects?"

The clerk allowed he didn't know what Longarm was talking about. Longarm didn't have reason to explain, so he didn't. He went over to the corner and sat down some more. He knew that the killer who'd planted that bomb was unlikely to be back before it failed to go off at midnight as planned. That gave him almost twelve hours to think about it. It was just as well. So far, he couldn't think of anything he could do about the sneaky son of a bitch. It seemed pretty obvious who was behind the attempt to shut up Aurora Stone in a mighty noisy way. That was the trouble with crooks. If half of 'em were as smart as they thought they were, the jail cells of these United States would hardly be half as crowded. Longarm was vexed with himself as well. For this was hardly the first time he'd made the mistake of expecting a crook to use a lick of common sense. The fact that Miss Aurora's boss had to be a blithering idiot wouldn't have done a thing for her if nobody had been nosy enough to find that bomb under her bed before it could plaster the ceiling with her shattered remains. The fact that the rascal who'd ordered it would have joined her in the great beyond shortly after wouldn't have done her a lick of good either. That the crazy son of a bitch had to be too rattled to be thinking straight didn't offer a lick of comfort. Longarm had long since learned, the hard way, that a stupid enemy could be the most dangerous. It was like trying to play checkers with a bratty kid who didn't know the rules and was as likely to jump you with one of your own checkers or, hell, a handy bottle cap. Longarm preferred his enemies smart enough to outwit. There was no way to outwit a half-wit because you could never count on him not setting fire to himself just to singe your eyebrows. Cockeyed Jack McCall hadn't had reason-one to gun old Hickok up in Deadwood that time, and had he had a lick of sense he'd have seen he was just going to get himself hung for the crime of sheer stupidity. But that hadn't done old Hickok any good when Cockeyed Jack had found himself facing Hickok's back with a gun and done what came natural to murderous morons. A lot of nonsense had been written, since, about how dumb old Hickok had been to turn his back to strangers as he took part in a friendly game of cards in the Number Ten Saloon. What nobody seemed to grasp was that Cockeyed Jack was *not* a stranger. Hickok's only mistake had been in assuming one of the back-room regulars with no reason on earth to back-shoot him cold-blooded in front of witnesses was about to do just that.

Longarm didn't even know the name of the crooked contractor Miss Aurora had been testifying against, let alone the details of the case. He made a mental note to get his own hands on a transcript of the trial, so far. That sweet little court stenographer, Miss Bubbles, would no doubt be willing to fix him up if he fixed her up again on the leather chesterfield in her office at the Federal Building. He might even get away with just a kiss and a promise, since there were limits to how long the widow woman up to Sherman Avenue would allow him to read in bed. That was the trouble with women. There was no way to get 'em to spread out more even. A man could go months without so much as a peck on the cheek and then there seemed to be more of 'em than he could shake his stick at. He knew as surely as he knew he'd never know why, that did he break up again with his old pal on Sherman Avenue, Miss Bubbles would run off and get married, Miss Morgana Floyd at the Arvada Orphan Asylum would be working nights, and that redhead at the Black Cat would shack up with her bald old boss. But let a man have one sure thing lined up for the coming sunset and it seemed every other gal in town felt honor-bound to make him the same tempting offer. There were times he suspected the unfair sex of confiding such matters to one another, despite how jealous they acted when a good old boy tried to be nice to all of 'em.

Ruminating on the mysteries of womankind, along with a light lunch and a lot more coffee in the hotel dining room while he had the time to kill, killed time until a little after two. Then he was just stuck, smoking in that same corner, wishing it was later.

But because he'd expected them to bring the witness back a lot closer to sundown, Longarm was pleasantly perked up when the same two gents brought her through the front door before three. She was holding a hankie to her teary face and they both looked mighty disgusted. As Longarm rose to greet them the one he knew said, "He beat the rap. You should have heard our boss cuss. But the infernal judge and dim-witted jury decided there wasn't enough evidence."

The federal agent on the far side of the weeping witness gal explained, "It boiled down to his word against the word of Miss Aurora, here, and them books kept in her own handwriting. The rascal lawyers intimated that hell hath no fury like a woman spurned and that she'd set him up with malice aforethought and account books she could have bought in any stationery store."

The brunette between them sobbed in anguish and insisted, "That's a horrid as well as barefaced lie! Mr. Porter and I were never romantically involved and I swear I only took him to the law because I was afraid I'd wind up in jail *with* him if I let him go on crooking the government like that!"

The man Longarm knew best patted her shoulder soothingly and assured her, "We know that, Miss Aurora. It was the judge and jury we couldn't sell your story to."

The other man who'd carried her home chimed in cheerfully with, "At least it's all over, now. You done your best. You may have even scared him back to honesty. I doubt he'll ever want to hire you back. But there's lots of jobs for a good bookkeeper."

She protested, "He'll *get* me, now that he's free as a bird to come after me, like he promised he would when I first confronted him with the figures. He said that if I turned him in he'd kill me slow and painful and, while I can't say much for his business ethics, I've always found Mr. Porter to be a man of his word!"

The cheerful one said, "Gents always threaten to do wonders and eat cucumbers when they feel rat-cornered, Miss Aurora. But, like I said, it's over now."

Longarm said quietly, "Let's not jump to hasty conclusions. I got something to show you." Then he took out the wad of tack-studded dynamite he'd put in a side pocket for safekeeping and added, "This might not have killed anyone *slow*, but it sure would have made a mess of this little lady. I found it under her bedsprings. Let's all go upstairs and I'll show you the clock and battery they'd put their time bomb together with."

Nobody argued about that. But as they were climbing up to the third story the two court agents were already starting to talk dumb. Their orders had been to carry Miss Aurora back here to the Rex and forget about her. The court had paid her rent to the end of the week and she was free to stay here that long, if she liked. But as far as Uncle Sam was concerned, Aurora Stone was on her own now.

Longarm could see how that made the teary-eyed little gal feel. So he said, flatly, "I work for Uncle Sam, too. I ain't about to toss this little lady out in the cold until I'm satisfied it's *safe* out there for an unescorted lady."

They got to Room 33. One of her now-reluctant escorts got out the key to open her door. Long-arm noticed he left the key in the lock. He didn't comment. He led all three to the bed table and picked up the still-ticking clock, saying, "It's a good thing Miss Aurora's own alarm clock had run

40

down. Whoever planted the dynamite under that bed must have figured a few extra ticks might not attract the attention of a lady getting ready for bed."

One of the other federal men picked up the dry cell, whistled, and said, "Looks new and fully charged. No way to trace such a common item, and that cheap clock they used as a timer could have come from almost anywhere."

Longarm nodded and said, "I had that figured a spell back. My point is that Miss Aurora here just told us her life had been threatened by one and only one man alone. If planting a bomb under a lady's bed doesn't constitute a serious threat, I don't know what does."

The one who'd been fooling with the cheap clock nodded and said, "This was set to detonate the infernal device at midnight. Nobody could have expected Porter to get off when they planted it. Even the judge was surprised as we were. The point is that nobody has any cause to kill this little lady, now."

Longarm blinked in surprise and raised his voice an octave to demand, "Are both of you asleep at the switch? I know you can't arrest her crooked boss again on charges he just beat. But can't you see attempted murder is another charge entire?"

The two court agents exchanged thoughtful glances. Then one said, "We'll ask our boss about it when we get back to the office. We had Porter figured as a crook to begin with, and this could hardly be the work of an honest businessman. Proving Porter was behind this attempt on Miss Aurora's life could be a problem, as picky as some

41

juries seem to be about material evidence. They let him off already, despite a pile of business ledgers in legible figures, adding up to outright fraud to anyone but that hayseed jury, just now. How are we supposed to convince another that Porter or even someone on his payroll had a thing to do with this cheap alarm clock? I don't see his signature on it anywhere, and I sort of doubt he'll admit to knowing a thing about it."

Before Longarm could work up a full head of steam they both assured him they'd do their best and asked for the dynamite as evidence as well. So he gave it to them, muttering, "You might tell the prosecutor, for me, that I think it's mighty low to leave any federal witness in this fix, after wringing all the use out of one and having no further use for the same."

They didn't argue. They may have agreed. But they had their orders and so, as they filed out, one suggested Longarm and the Justice Department were free to guard Miss Aurora all they might want to. Then they left him there to work it out with the witness they had no further interest in. She somehow wound up facedown across her bed, crying fit to bust. Longarm took the key from her door, pocketed it, and shut the door, making certain of the latch, before he moved over to the bed, sat down beside her, and placed a comforting hand on her heaving shoulders, saying, "Aw, come on, it ain't that bad, Miss Aurora."

She sobbed, "They're going to kill me! I just know it! And nobody cares!"

He assured her soberly, "I care, ma'am. So kindly turn off the water works and let's see if the two of us, together, can't outfox one total idiot."

She rolled on one elbow to face him, dabbing at her eyes as she choked back a sob to say, "Mr. Porter isn't an idiot. He's slick and mean as a snake. There's no telling how much bran and dog food he'd have sold to the B.I.A. as Indian grub if I hadn't gotten to wondering, keeping his very books, how come he was buying pig fodder and selling flour and corned beef we'd never been billed for."

Longarm shrugged and said, "If the poor Indians ate the evidence and that jury didn't buy your bookkeeping, what's done is done. They tried Cockeyed Jack McCall twice on the same charge. But, as a rule, the Constitution doesn't allow that. Your ex-boss is free and clear, until he does it again. I want you to study on that, Miss Aurora. You say this Porter gent is slick as well as shifty. I hope you've read him right. For, if you have, right now he ought to be sweating bullets."

She stared at him more in wonder than in hope. So he explained, "This mattress under us was set to bump against the ceiling later tonight. I don't see how he could know I found the infernal device and defused it. So, as things now stand, old Porter has just walked free, aims to say that way, and expects to hear a lady who presents no further danger to him to go boomp in the night."

She gulped and said, "I told you he was awfully mean."

"I doubt he's half as mad at you right now. His best bet, and let's hope he knows it, would be to let the whole thing just die down. You say he's smart, and nobody but a fool would want a needless murder investigation, with him high on the list of suspects. So, hoping I'm playing checkers with

43

someone as knows the rules, I'd say his next move will be to recover that bomb he still thinks he has ticking under us right now. He knows he has until midnight. He doesn't know I'm on to him. So let's study on how we can trap him or, more likely, a nervous gun waddy he has on his payroll. I know it couldn't have been Porter in the flesh as tried to upset me earlier this very day. He was in court with you at the time. Do you know how nervous someone *else* working for him might have been while you were still keeping the books?"

She frowned thoughtfully and decided, "Mr. Porter had some sort of tough-talking men working in his warehouse down by the Burlington yards. I hardly ever went there, myself. I caught him cheating on paper. I don't recall anyone acting all that tense, though. Is that important?"

He shrugged and said, "Probably not. It's one thing to hire a man to tote feed sacks for you and another thing entire to ask him to kill folk for you. We're likely discussing one or more hired killers, at least one of 'em sort of hair-triggered."

She blanched and curled up to cry some more. So Longarm took her in his arms to assure her, soothingly, "He ain't after you now. I'm after him, but he doesn't know it. If he has a lick of sense he'll send someone to sneak in here and slip that bomb out from under this bed before midnight. At least an hour before midnight if he sends his nervous nelly."

She felt softer and smelled better in his arms than he'd expected, pretty as she was. But she stiffened and cast an anxious glance at the door, over his shoulder. He said, "The door's well bolted and I just told you Porter has more use for

44

you alive than otherwise, now that he's been found not guilty of the charges you brung against him. They know we're up here if they've been watching the front entrance worth mention, and I'm sure they have been. They knew just where I was supposed to be sitting earlier today."

She relaxed in his arms a mite, but asked in a worried tone, "Then how do they mean to recover their own device without hurting anybody, if they know we're up here?"

"They have until midnight," he said. "They're hoping we'll go out for supper, at least, before then."

She stiffened some more and said, "Let's walk out the front door right now, then!"

But he held her steady—she sure was a wriggly little thing—and said, "Not yet. Two reasons. It's too early in the day for supper and we have to wait until my relief man shows up. They'll see him leave, since Uncle Sam don't seem as worried about you, now. Then they'll see you and me leave as well, and I mean to take you clean out of the neighborhood for supper at Romano's Italian eatery near Cherry Creek. If they tail us they'll see us inhaling noodles and red wine a good ways off. *That's* when they'll sneak someone in here to recover the bomb, and guess who'll be waiting for 'em?"

She gasped, giggled, and told him he was ever so smart. So he kissed her. It seemed the natural thing to do, after hanging on to her sweet squirms this long. She kissed back, in a way that assured him her recent social life had been sort of limited. But as they came up for air, she blushed and de-

45

manded, "Is this the way you usually guard a witness, sir?"

He said, "My folks named me Custis. I don't know why, either. If you don't want me kissing you, just say so. My main intent has been to keep you from running about in circles, and that kissing just sort of snuck up on me."

She flung an arm around the back of his neck and said, "Me, too." And so this time, when they kissed, he got rid of his hat and lowered her to the bed covers to kiss her right. She seemed to like it until his free hand got to wandering, with a sort of mind of its own, and she crossed her bare thighs on it once it had crept above her garters, and warned him in an unconvincing tone that they didn't have time for that sort of intimacy. So he kissed her some more and worked his hand higher before he asked innocently, "How much intimacy did you have in mind? It can't be much after three, and my relief man don't figure to show up before six or later."

That made her laugh too much to pay attention to his questing hand until she suddenly noticed where it was, now, and protested, "Oh, good heavens, just what do you think you're doing to my privates, sir?" Then she spread her thighs wider and moaned, "I mean Custis, I guess," as he got his fingers inside her underdrawers and commenced to rock the boy in the boat for her with gentle skill, murmuring, "Just trying to find out if another lady up on Sherman Avenue still loves me."

The one he was loving-up in the Rex Hotel naturally demanded further explanation to that odd remark. So he said he was just funning and sort of forgot about it himself, until the next thing he knew Aurora gasped, "Oh, my God, you . . . you're having your wicked way with me!"

It didn't feel all that wicked to him, even though they both had their pants on, sort of. For she sure felt nice and naked where he had his own bare self, and it was her suggestion, once they'd climaxed together in formal attire, that he let her at least take her underdrawers off, for land's sake, before they got all messy. So he helped her out of them and, as long as they were at it, peeled off everything else but her silk stockings and high-button shoes. She let him. She couldn't have stopped him. But as he shucked beside her atop the covers, she covered her perky bare breasts with her palms and protested it was broad daylight and that she wasn't a damnit Greek statue on public view. But he assured her she was built better than any marble statue he'd ever done this to and, once he was doing it to her, right, she giggled and informed him archly that she felt sure he'd treat a statue just as fresh, if it was at all willing.

He didn't argue. It was likely the pure truth, even though he'd never tried to tear a marble fig leaf off a lady in an art museum. For though some were built mighty tempting, Longarm preferred something warmer than marble in his arms, and though this one's last name might be Stone, she sure was soft and warm as any man might want, and she kissed just swell with her lips as well. So it was a good thing Longarm had rewound and set the alarm clock still on the premises. Deputy Flynn might have been shocked as hell when he turned up if that alarm hadn't gone off just as

47

Longarm and Aurora were getting around to the really dirty stuff.

He'd given them an hour's lead on Flynn. So they had time to finish, that way, and even wash up a mite in the adjoining bath before they went down to the lobby to wait for Longarm's supper-time relief. Aurora was seated in that corner chair and Longarm was pacing and muttering a mite when Deputy Flynn showed up a few minutes later. Flynn ticked his hat brim at the lady but told Longarm, "You're off and so am I. The boss just sent me to tell you there's no further need to guard the lady as a witness, now that the trial is over."

Longarm growled, "I heard about Porter walking free. We ain't done with him, yet." Then he quickly filled his junior deputy in on the other details. Flynn agreed that while Billy Vail had left for the day it seemed sensible to set a trap for anyone with such disgusting habits. So they quickly worked out a plan of action that even Aurora found just about foolproof. The three of them left together. When they got to the corner the two deputies shook as if they were parting for the night. Then, as Flynn mosied off to gather up some of the other boys, sneak in the back way, and stake out Aurora's room, Longarm hailed a passing hack and hired them a ride to Romano's. As they rode off seated side by side, Aurora giggled and said, "Anyone watching will no doubt think you're sparking me, off duty, you fresh thing."

To which he had to answer honestly, "I don't have a rep for being prim and proper. Do you? I want you to study on that before you answer."

She frowned and whispered, lest their driver hear, "Is that any sort of question to ask a lady you insisted on loving in broad day, damnit?"

He murmured soothingly, "I ain't talking about how well we know each other, now. Your boss accused you in open court of being a woman scorned. Might he have any call to consider you sort of warm-natured, honey?"

She snapped, "Of course not! It was he who fondled my derriere one afternoon when I first came to work for him, as a matter of fact. I assured him in no uncertain terms that I was not a woman to mix business with pleasure. After that he never even tried to get fresh again. Why do you ask?"

"Covering all bets. I'm glad you handled him as a woman of the world, rather than a fussy spinster who might not go to supper with me on such short notice. Did you ever go out with anyone else while you were working for Porter?"

She looked away and said, "I may have. A working girl has a right to have gentlemen friends. You're the first man who's ever had his way with me on such short notice, if that's what you're so concerned about."

He assured her he was more concerned about the way her having supper with him might look to anyone tailing them. Then they were having supper at Romano's and enjoying it. She said it was a swell joint and asked for second helpings. He encouraged her to linger over coffee and dessert as well. So it was good and dark by the time they'd finished and he led her out the back door by way of the kitchen. The Romano family were old pals who were used to Longarm's odd ways. In the gritty dark alley out back she asked him where on earth he was taking her. He explained, "To some other pals of mine who can hide you out for the night. I hope you don't dislike Chinese folk. You'll find the bed linens clean as anything, it being a Chinese laundry and all."

She laughed incredulously and said, "I thought we were going back to my hotel, as soon as it was safe, dear."

"It won't be safe this side of midnight. It might not be all that safe after if we don't catch anyone sneaking into your room there. I'll just bed you down with the Wang Fongs and sneak back to the Rex myself. We'll know better in the morning just how safe you are, even in a Chinese laundry."

"Surely you and your friends will have caught the bomber by then," she said.

"If he shows up. If he don't, it'll mean old Porter just ain't worried about your health and we'll have a whole new checker game, won't we?"

Chapter 4

That was the way things worked out. Longarm joined Flynn, Smiley and Dutch in the room across from Aurora's before midnight. When a neighborhood church bell chimed twelve times and nary a soul had evidenced any interest in Room 33, Longarm swore and told his pals, "That tears it. Nobody's about to come and defuse a bomb that should have just gone off. All I have to work out now is whether Porter's still after his ex-bookkeeper or just doesn't give a shit. She's safe for the moment, and I can see you boys are mad enough at me. So I thank you for your help and we'll talk about it some more during regular office hours, if I come up with anything."

They all agreed he'd been sort of dumb, so far, and split up to wend their separate ways. Longarm considered wending back to Wang Fong's. But he

51

knew the walls of their frame shack were thin and that Aurora couldn't make love silently, once she got to making love at all. So, seeing she was snug and safe for the night, he decided he'd best wend on up to Sherman Avenue and cover that base while he had the time to spare.

The widow woman seemed sore about something when she finally came to her door in her nightgown with her light brown hair down for bed. She told him he had some nerve darkening her door at this ungodly hour and demanded, "What happened? Did that sassy barmaid at the Black Cat have a headache?"

He chuckled fondly and assured her, truthfully enough when one studied on it, that he hadn't been anywhere near the Black Cat that evening and that he'd been stuck on a stakeout most of the night. So she relented and let him in. But, being curious, once he'd been in her a while, she naturally wanted to know what he might have been expecting all this time at some infernal hotel.

He moved in her teasingly as he assured her, "Nothing fine as this, sweet stuff. Did anyone ever tell you how much you resemble a Greek statue with your duds off? Not one of them slim Diana gals. More like, say, old Venus or Juno. It's sure a wonder how many swell ways you goddess gals can curve, each mighty yummy in her own different way."

"I know I'm good in bed," she said. "Just keep doing what you know I like and tell me who you were after all this time if it wasn't another woman."

He told her tersely he'd been laying for a mad bomber, without going into the intended victim. Then they got too excited for idle conversation for a spell and, once they came back down from the stars she just yawned, bless her, and told him not to get his fool self blown up before Billy Vail could manage to get him killed by the rurales.

That was when Longarm got to show how smart he could be. He started to assure her he'd been taken off that detail for now. Then he wondered why any gent in his position would want to say a dumb thing like that. For, if he worked it right, he might just manage to convince this gal he was out of town instead of with another one and, whether she was in real danger or not, old Aurora was built so different and moved so different that he was inspired to start all over with the more voluptuous widow woman, who laughed with girlish glee and confided that she was ready to buy his excuse after all, seeing he was just too horny right now to have been cheating on her earlier.

That was the way some gals put it. Longarm felt sort of insulted by the term. For he hardly ever cheated at cards and made no false promises to any gal. None of them, damnit, owned him, and he assumed they liked him for having such a romantic nature.

He awoke before her in the cold gray dawn and got dressed to slip out before she could wake up and say more cold things to him. Billy Vail was thundergasted to find Longarm waiting for him on the steps of the Federal Building, full of beans and ready to go. As they went upstairs to open the office for the day Longarm brought Vail up to date on the latest attempt against Aurora Stone. Billy agreed her ex-boss sounded like an infernal pest. But once he had Longarm seated and smoking in the inner office, Vail explained, "We're just too shorthanded to

53

stomp every piss-ant west of the Big Muddy, old son. That witness gal ain't our row to hoe, now that the Porter case has turned out so dismal. Your concern about her does you credit. But we have a heap of more dangerous rascals to round up, so—"

"So what do you call a man who'd blow a lady up with dynamite studded with carpet tacks, a disorderly drunk?" Longarm cut in with a puzzled scowl.

"I'd call Porter a gent running scared. He must have felt sure he was on his way to Leavenworth. I know *we* were. Death threats spoken in panic ain't likely to be carried out by a man sobering up after a victory celebration. I know for a fact Porter and some pals spent most of last night at Emma Gould's house of ill repute. Madam Emma told us so. So Porter has a perfect alibi. Police informants know better than to fib to us about attempted murder."

Longarm blew smoke out his nostrils like a vexed bull and insisted, "Of *course* the son of a bitch would want to set himself up with an alibi for the time Aurora Stone went boom. My point is that they could have tried to save her and they never."

Vail bit the tip off his own cigar and spat it on the rug he forbade Longarm to get ashes on. Then he said, "They outguessed you. Sending a henchman into even a possible trap might have struck Porter as being riskier than letting her just die. It ain't as if he could be all that *fond* of a gal who came close to putting him in prison. But, like I said, by now he's no doubt nursing a hangover and losing interest in the little gal. He has to know that bomb never went off. So, assuming he has the brains of a gnat, he knows someone found it in time and couldn't care less. For the gal can never bear witness against him, now that the prosecution has shot her wad."

"Billy, the man told her he was going to kill her, and last night he *tried* to."

Vail shrugged and said, "Porter knows what he said, and he knows she's told us about his death threat. He knows that he'll have to answer all sorts of tedious questions if she even sprains her ankle. So if he's smart he won't go anywhere near her from now on."

"What if he's dumb?" asked Longarm. "The one they sent to gun me at the hotel was wild and un-professional, you know."

Billy Vail nodded sagely and said, "I've been studying on that. Amarillo Jack threw down on you wild and woolly, *before* you'd been posted to guard witness-one against a slick businessman like old Porter. That business with infernal machines strikes me as the work of a cunning criminal. Has it oc-curred to you that the two trigger-happy rascals after you could have nothing to do with Miss Au-rora Stone? You were nowhere near her when old Amarillo Jack tried to kill you. Had the one with the scattergun nailed you in the lobby, with the gal you were guarding nowhere near you—"

"I follow your drift," Longarm cut in, chewing his cheroot ferociously. "That's all I need. Two sets of killers entire to worry about. I reckon I'll just have me a private talk with old Amarillo Jack."

Vail nodded but said, "They won't let you pistol-whip him much at County General. I've been squir-rel-caging my brain about that notion to send you down to Juarez with him. On the one hand it's mighty risky, and good help is hard to find these days. On the other hand, like I said before, it fig-ures to be a long train ride in a private compartment. What are *your* thoughts on the matter, old son?"

Longarm grimaced and replied, "The rurales make me nervous. So does the notion of some rascal I don't know sending one hired gun after another to do me dirty. No man's luck can last forever, and I'd sure like to get them before they get me. How much time do I have to study on it, boss?"

"Amarillo Jack's fool leg is still in traction. He may be able to travel in a day or so. What did you have in mind?"

Longarm got back to his feet and adjusted his gun belt to ride handier as he growled, "That gives me just a day or more to make sure Miss Aurora's out of danger for keeps. So with your permission, I'd best get cracking."

They told him at Porter's office on Market Street that the boss was likely over at their warehouse in Butchertown by the Burlington yards. So that was where Longarm went next. Butchertown wasn't as much a town as a state of mind or a smell. It had no exact borders and wasn't on any map of Denver. Like other such ugly districts it just sort of spread like a fungus from around the railroad stockyards. Denver being where most of the stock ranging a heap of Colorado wound up.

It wasn't bragged on much by the gents dressed cow in many a downtown saloon, but Denver shipped more *sheep* than any other town west of the Big Muddy, albeit Utah was catching up with Colorado on sheep these days. But they still punched a lot of cows aboard at Denver, and while most beef and mutton was still sent east alive 'f not well, a heap was slaughtered and processec on the premises. So aside from the slaughterhouses themselves, a mess of secondary industries had sprung up all around to take a cut of the meat pie. There were tanneries, lard rendering plants, outfits as made tallow candles, soap and such from the leftovers of lard renderers, and of course the leather working that went on cheek by jowl with the stinky but handy tanneries. Nothing stunk worse than the neighborhood glue factories, unless it was the fertilizer farms where sheep- and cowshit got to dry in the sun and thin air of the Mile High City, as Denver liked to call its fool self. Warehouses holding all the above for shipping wholesale were tucked in anywhere there was still space. The big one owned and operated by old Sidney Porter was between a glue factory and five acres of pent-up bawling sheep. So it was just as well there were no windows cut through the sides of the big brick cube. The cavernous front entrance gaped open to inhale such air as they might need inside. As Longarm headed into it he was told by a tough-looking jasper lounging against a doorjamb with his gun hung low and tied down, that he couldn't come in. Had he said it politely, Longarm would have shown him his badge and I.D. But since the guard or whatever added insult to injury, Longarm felt obliged to punch him in the jaw and then beat him to the draw as he lay there cussing and spitting tobacco juice and blood.

That naturally attracted considerable attention from inside. But since Longarm was looming tall as well as armed and dangerous over their fallen comrade, the handful of raggedy warehousemen and one pompous specimen in a three-piece business suit and pearl Stetson approached with hands

57

polite and looks of poker-faced curiosity, however they might have felt about the odd manners of Longarm.

The one dressed up for church stopped just out of pistol-whip range to inquire, softly, "How come you just put one of my boys on his ass, pilgrim?"

To which Longarm replied in as reasonable a tone, "He called me a dumb son of a bitch. I don't mind a man intimating I'm dumb, as long as he can prove it. But there's something about being called a son of a bitch that just brings out the natural beast in me."

By this time the one Longarm had downed was getting back up, keeping his hands well clear of his tied-down S&W. The obvious boss told him, "Go dab some branch water on that lip, Barky." And, as Longarm's victim vanished in the gloom, the fancy dresser smiled at Longarm and confided, "We call him Barky because he flares up easy. I'm a heap more polite. So would you mind putting that gun away and telling me what you want?"

Longarm identified himself and said he was looking for the one and original Sid Porter. The priss winced and replied, "You have found him. Only my friends call me Sidney and my employees call me Mr. Porter."

Longarm smiled thinly and said, "It's a good thing I don't work for you, ain't it, Sid? As you ought to have guessed by now, me being of the federal persuasion, I have come to have a word with you about the trouble you just got out of, some damned way."

Porter's beefy and likely once-handsome face turned a deeper shade of pink as he snapped, "The case is closed. I was cleared on every charge. My lawyers say I don't have to ever talk about that trouble again, with anyone, unless and until you nosy, ah, gentlemen, have another charge entire to accuse me and mine of."

Longarm nodded soberly and said, "I know. I think the Constitution is just swell as it is. I ain't here to talk about the books Miss Aurora Stone was keeping for you. I'm here to talk about her in the flesh. I hope you understand that bruising a square inch of the same would constitute another charge entire?"

Porter frowned and proclaimed, "That lying little sass don't work for me no more. I'd be lying, myself, if I said I wished her well, after all the trouble and expense she just put me through. But do I look like a man who would strike a woman?"

Longarm had been studying on that. Porter had one of those baby-kissing politician's faces that read honest and upright and square until one studied those beady blue eyes. Longarm said, "I doubt anyone is out to beat the little lady up, Sid. Lucky for her, I found the bomb some abusive bastard planted in her room at the Palace Hotel before it could go off."

The trap didn't work, either way, when Porter replied with a puzzled frown, "I thought she was staying at the Rex as a guest of Uncle Sam. You say someone planted a bomb in her room? Where?"

Longarm sighed and said, "I'd sure hate to play checkers with you for money. The lady tells us that long before I found her bed set to blow up just after she got in it around ten you'd made a few remarks about her winding up dead if she testified against you in court, as we both know she did."

The oily rascal's eyes didn't even flicker at the

deliberate mismention of the bomb's timing mechanism. Porter smiled so sincerely it made Longarm want to hit him and said, "Let's go on back to my office. I can see we have some things to set straight."

Longarm followed him. As they passed through aisles of stacked bags and boxes he asked the wholesaler, in as casual a tone as he could manage, whether he was still vending to the federal government. Porter stopped, whirled around red-faced indeed, and almost bawled, "You know damned well I'm not! Thanks to that lying bitch both my army and B.I.A. contracts have been set aside until further notice, even though I just *beat* her insane and spiteful charges!"

As Longarm just smiled at him, uncommitted either way, Porter cussed, tore open a pasteboard box, and hauled out a big tin can to thrust it in Longarm's face, snarling, "Here's one of the very cans of corned beef she put down as dog food in those shifty records she compiled against me. I ask you, does this look like dog food? Read the damned label. Open the can if you like!"

Longarm took the can in one hand and reached for his pocketknife with the other. He read the label and mused aloud, "Well, it sure does say there's sixteen ounces of canned corned beef inside. How come it says said beef was corned and canned in old Mexico, of all places?"

As Longarm proceeded to open the can with the can-opener blade of his handy pocketknife, Porter explained in an innocent tone, "I bought it from an American-owned Mex cannery because they gave me the best price, of course. I make no bones about buying as cheap and selling as dear as I can manage.

It's the Yankee way of doing business and there's not one law against it."

By this time Longarm had pried open the lid. He sniffed, got out a taste of the contents with his knife blade, and gave it an objective chaw before he nodded soberly and said, "Well, it sort of smells like corned beef and it sort of tastes like corned beef. But I've never eaten much dog food."

Porter snapped, "It's not dog food, damnit! They were raising beef in Mexico before the first Texas cowboy yipped. You don't have to be an Irishman to know how to make corned beef, damnit. The Irish learned to like the stuff on this side of the water. You just pickle the beef a spell before you go ahead and can it regular. If you can it fresh off the cow you wind up with what the English call bully beef. It don't taste as good. I was doing them damned Indians a *favor* by shipping 'em such swell stuff."

Longarm didn't know what to do with the rest of the can. So he handed it to Porter as he folded his knife and put it away, asking, "What about the bran you were accused of selling as flour?"

Porter put the can atop the opened box for someone else to worry about as he explained, "That was an honest mix-up. The mill sent us whole wheat flour instead of the white flour we ordered. I'll allow there must have been some bran in it. That's how come they call it whole wheat. I'll allow I went and shipped some to the Arapaho Agency and, all right, I didn't think they'd notice or care about the difference. It was perfectly good flour. How was I to know the infernal redskins put flour instead of sugar in their coffee and insisted it be just as white?"

Longarm chuckled at the picture and said, "If all

61

this jawing about past misunderstandings is designed to get me off the track, you're wasting your time, Sid. We both know you can't be tried twice, no matter how good or bad them government rations were. I would like to get back to the threats you made against a lady who sure seems to be threatened."

Porter called Aurora a trouble-making lunatic all the way back to his corner cubbyhole. Then he offered Longarm a bentwood rocker, sat down at his rolltop desk, and got out a pint of bourbon as he grumbled, "I never told her I meant to kill her *physical*. I warned her she was dead as a bookkeeper, professionally, if she went to the law with her wild suspicions. Would you be willing to hire a bookkeeper knowing she'd got her last boss in trouble? Bookkeepers are damnit supposed to keep the boss *out* of trouble, not get him *into* it."

Longarm allowed Miss Aurora was likely more idealistic than some, as Porter poured two heroic drinks and handed one to him. It was good stuff. Longarm felt obliged to say so. Porter sighed and gulped his own drink down entire before he sort of whined, "I swear I don't know what got into that crazy gal. I paid her the going wages and I never once told her to write down anything shady."

To which Longarm had to reply with a chuckle, "You should have instructed her better, then. She claims she just put down what came in and what went out and didn't notice what you were up to for a spell."

Porter winced as if he'd been bee stung and insisted, "She did no such thing. She doctored them books to make me look bad on her own. Do you think I'd be dumb enough to hire someone to record my misdeeds if I was misdeeding, damnit?"

"We're talking in circles again," Longarm said. "You already managed to convince a federal court that Miss Aurora was a dumb bookkeeper. What was that guff about her calling you a crook because she was a woman scorned? How come you scorned her, if you did? She ain't that bad-looking."

Porter shrugged and said modestly, "Neither am I. I like to kiss women as much as the next man, and I'll allow I might have been tempted now and again. But I try not to mix business with pleasure. I hired her to keep my books for me. When I pay for ass I don't do so during business hours. She was a flirty little sass, and I'll allow I may have flirted back. But nothing ever come of it and the next thing I knew she flared up at me one night at my business office and started accusing me of all sorts of things."

Porter helped himself to another jolt without offering Longarm another. He consumed it and went on. "I told her she was crazy. I warned her I'd see she never got another job in these parts if she persisted in her madness. I told her that working in our main office she'd never even seen the stuff rolling in and out of this warehouse, and that it was her dumb word against mine and all the boys working here. Look, I even offered her a *raise* if she'd just let me show her where she'd gone wrong with her facts and figures. But, as you know, she insisted on taking me to the law and, as I warned her, I beat her charges. So if she's still saying mean things about me, it only goes to show how much she hates me for no good reason at all!"

Since he couldn't drink any more, Longarm hauled out a cheroot and lit it while he collected his thoughts. Then he blew smoke at Porter and said,

"You're good. You tell a mighty plausible story, and I've had my own troubles with spiteful women. I'll allow they don't always need a sensible motive to do a man dirt and find themselves out of a job and blacklisted. So I'd be sorely tempted to write Miss Aurora off as the confused young gal you claim she is, if only someone hadn't backed up her story by almost killing her last night."

Porter protested, "Is it engraved in rock that I have to be the only gent with reason to dislike her? How do you know she didn't do someone *else* as dirty? Lord knows she did *me* dirty enough! Thanks to her I'm out a whopping legal fee and I've lost some good government contracts as well!"

Longarm nodded knowingly and said, "We talked about other possible enemies over supper, last night. She told me she went straight to work for you when she got here from Omaha less'n a year ago. You hired her right off, as you know, because she'd had experience with a big meat packer there and could prove it with good references."

Porter nodded but said, "Of course I hired her, damnit. To keep my records proper, not to get me thrown in jail or bankrupt. My point is that she failed to ruin me. So I've no further call to ever even mention her name again. You ought to study on who *else* she might have mean-mouthed in her travels! The lying little bitch is mean as hell!"

Longarm got back to his feet as he said, "She didn't act all that mean to me. She hasn't worked for anyone else here in Denver. So guess who I mean to question further if any harm comes to one hair on her head? Like the Indian chief said, I have spoken."

As he strode out and headed for the front entrance, Porter tagged along after him, saying as sincerely as he could manage that he didn't even want to find one hair of the lady's head on his serge suit. He asked just as innocently where Miss Aurora might be staying if she wasn't at the Rex. In the doorway Longarm turned to favor him with a sober stare as he said, "If you don't know where she is you won't be able to get at her. Take my fatherly advice and don't try."

When he picked Aurora up at the Chinese laundry he found her more than ready to go most anywhere, even though she allowed the Wang Fongs had treated her like a long-lost daughter. She said being treated as a Chinese daughter took some getting used to. The kids were cute but there was a limit to how many she enjoyed in her lap at the same time. As he walked her along the alley she asked where they were headed. He told her, "Far side of Cherry Creek. We can cross her without using any bridges with the summer so dry. I made sure nobody followed me from Porter's warehouse, but they might know where I usually room on the less-fashionable side of the creek. I'll carry you over any water you can't jump in them high buttons."

She kept walking, but objected that she didn't know anyone in such a disreputable neighborhood. He said, "I assumed as much. Let's hope they do as well. As long as we don't go near my disreputable rooming house they ain't likely to search for an out-of-town lady of fashion in a slum. The place I'm taking you to is a hidey-hole I've used in the past to, ah, hide out a witness. It's over a stable owned by a discreet Mex I know. From out front you'd never notice there's a four-room flat built under the peaked roof. It's kept clean and you ain't tall enough for the low overhead to worry you."

She hugged his arm tighter and purred, "I doubt I'll get to stand up all that much, once you get me there, lover. But how long do you expect to hide me out, for heaven's sake?"

"Just 'til we make sure nobody's trying to kill you. I put that to Sid Porter sort of firm, just now. He says he was only funning when he offered to kill you that time."

She grimaced and said, "He lied about a lot of other things. But we've agreed that bomb must have been planted to shut me up while his trial was still in progress. Now that he's somehow gotten off, and knows you suspect him, what motive might he have for taking further risks against me, dear?"

"He just mentioned that. If nobody ever took dumb revenge there'd be a lot less work for gents like me. He admitted that you'd damaged his business, even though he'd made a fibber of you and your records in court. He's going to want those government contracts back as soon as your accusations blow over. He knows you're still accusing him. He knows you're likely to keep calling him a crook as long as you're alive. The question before the house is which risk worries him the most. While he makes up his mind, I don't want anyone but me to know where you are and how to get at you."

She didn't argue with that chain of logic until they'd sandbar hopped Cherry Creek and made it to the hideout he'd chosen, by way of more back alleyways. But when he had her up in the four small rooms above the Sepulvada stable she shot him an arch look, and said, "It is nice and cozy up here. Are you sure you didn't just want to sort of shack up with me, you horny thing? Sooner or later I have to start looking for another job, you know."

He smiled down at her and said, "Late sounds safer than sooner. Make yourself at home while I run over to the house and tell fibs to old Pete Sepulvada. He'll send one of his kids to fetch us all the provisions we need. There's running water and a coal stove in the kitchen. There's no need to tell even Sepulvada that I ain't just shacked up here with some otherwise unimportant gal. The less anyone knows, the safer you'll be here, see?"

She smiled at him thoughtfully and replied, "I see you've had other, ah, witnesses of my gender here before."

He didn't answer as he ducked back down the steep stairway. He didn't like to lie, even though that did seem the best way to deal with it. There was no reason at all to tell old Aurora how he'd found this place, after the time he and that warm-natured Mex gal had busted the bedsprings at his regular rooming house and his landlady had made such a fuss about his digs being single occupancy.

He found old Sepulvada weeding out back and it only took a few words and a twenty-dollar gold piece to work things out with the laconic old Mex. So Longarm went back up to tell Aurora they were good for a week and that the provisions he'd just ordered would be left on the stairs in case he was out. Then he stared thoughtfully down at her and added, "Are you that sleepy already?"

She smiled coyly up at him from under the bed sheet she'd thrown over her nude charms to reply, demurely, that she wasn't the least bit sleepy. He started to point out that it wasn't nearly noon yet and that he was supposed to be on duty. But he

67

didn't want to upset her. So as he shucked his own duds to get under the sheet with her he observed, "Just a quick cuddle, then. I can't hardly investigate crimes in this position, sweet as it may be."

Thanks to having spent the wee small hours with another gal, a quick one seemed out of the question. But she took his hard-to-keep-hard efforts as evidence of protracted passion and seemed to enjoy them. He began to enjoy them more once he'd thrown the sheet down to get down to business, since her business looked so much different than the same parts of the widow woman up to Sherman Avenue. There was a lot to be said for that heathen Turkish harem notion, even though it was small wonder the Turks never seemed to get much *else* done. When at last he managed an exhausted ejaculation in her totally different charms, Longarm collapsed weakly down in her arms and panted, "I suspect the Ottoman Empire just declined some more. I'd rather do that some more than anything else I can think of. But unless I do some serious thinking I'll have to hide you here forever."

She purred she might not mind that. But he got up, ducked into the bath for a quick rub-down with a damp rag, and came back to sit on the edge of the bed and dress up to go hunting as he told her, "I noticed Porter buys some of his goods down Mexico way. What can you tell me about that, honey?"

She shrugged a bare shoulder and replied, "I saw bills of lading from all over. I'd need my books to give you the names of his Mexican suppliers, and the federal prosecutor never gave them back to me, the mean thing."

As he hauled on a boot he explained, "Porter's own business records are his to keep and cherish, now that they're no longer evidence. The court may have a transcript I can get a peek at if I ask nice." Then he blinked and added, "There's lots of ways to get a look at court records, and most lawyers know more ways than I might. When they told you they'd be guarding you at that hotel, might my name have come up in conversation?"

She pursed her lips earnestly in thought before she told him she just couldn't recall, adding, "They did assure me they'd have the most reliable deputies from the marshal's office guarding me around the clock when I wasn't in court. I don't think they told me any names, though. Is it important, dear?"

"It could be, if they made up their list before even my boss, Billy Vail, was asked. I don't like to brag, but I am his senior deputy and I'd sure like to post me to such a vital chore if I wasn't the one getting stuck with it. At least one of the gun hands sent after me, personal, is known to have his own Mex connections. It sure is a small world, ain't it?"

He went to the door, opened it to find a couple of boxes of provisions, and toted them into the bitty kitchen off the combined bed and living room as Aurora followed him, naked as a jay. He leaned her bare bottom against the sink to kiss her good before he told her, "I'll likely be back around sundown. If I ain't, just hang tough and don't worry about me. I'll likely be aboard a train with a prisoner. I may have to spend a day or more south of the border, looking into the canning business down yonder. Our land-lord will put more vittles outside the door from time to time. You don't have to talk to him and he won't want to talk to you until our room and board runs out."

She snuggled her bare body against his tweed

suit, demanding in a worried voice to know what she should do if he failed to return at all. He patted her nude spine reassuringly and told her, "I don't know. I mean to get back sooner, if I can. If I can't it'll likely mean we're both in a hell of a mess."

Chapter 5

Amarillo Jack looked worn out by the train ride already as the southbound D&RG chugged out of the Denver yards. Longarm and his prisoner were seated opposite one another in a dinky private compartment at one end of a Pullman car. The uncouth youth he'd shot in the thigh was naturally wearing one boot and one plaster cast from hip to bare toes under the larger sized hospital pants they'd managed to get him into. The rest of him was wearing the hickory shirt and battered Stetson he'd been wearing when Longarm sent him to the hospital. It would have been dumb to give him back his gun rig or the bowie he'd been packing in his boot.

Longarm waited 'til the train was rolling good across the tawny prairie with a view of the lavender Front Range to their right before he got out two cheroots, lit them both, and handed one to his prisoner, saying, "We got some time and miles to spend with one another. So let's get a few things straight, Jack. The rule book says I'm to keep your ankles in leg irons and one of your wrists cuffed to the arm of that seat you're perched on at all times. I don't see how you can run any faster with one leg in a cast than an average prisoner in leg irons might. I will have to cuff you after dark if I get sleepy. Otherwise, it might be best for both of us if you was free to use the commode under that low table next to you whenever you need to. I ain't about to unbutton your pants myself. They'll be feeding us first class before you can starve to death. I told the porter we won't want the bunks made up in here. One night dozing upright won't hurt either of us and we'll be getting off at El Paso at an ungodly hour in any case. So why get undressed in the first place? Are you following me so far, old son?"

Amarillo Jack took a drag on his own cheroot, nodded sullenly, and muttered, "I sure wish I wasn't following you to *Mexico*, you bastard."

Longarm smiled thinly across at him to say, "Don't cuss at me. I'm only going to say that once. Now I want you to pay close attention, Jack. I am a lawman of the old school. I've read the dumb things they write about reform being better than punishment, and I still think there's nothing like some punishing to convince boys like you to reform. In your case they could let you make pot holders and play indoor ball games for a hundred years without it reforming you worth spit. So I hope you understand that I don't treat prisoners decent because I'm a big sissy. You act sensible with me and I'll not rawhide you. If you make one move I find at all suspicious, I'll kill you. I've a warrant to deliver you

72

dead or alive. I don't give a shit either way. It's as simple as that."

Amarillo Jack choked back another remark about Longarm's ancestry and muttered, "Don't tempt me. I knew your rep when they sent me after you. If I had two good legs to run with I'd as soon take my chances with flying lead as a damned old Mexican rope dance. What you're doing to me is inhuman and you know it."

Longarm stared out at the scenery a spell before he chuckled and said, "My boss, Marshal Vail, said he figured the prospects of meeting your maker down Mexico way might persuade you to make a better deal for yourself. I told him he was full of it, of course."

They both let some scenery roll by for a time. Then Amarillo Jack asked, quietly, "What kind of a deal?"

Longarm took another drag on his smoke and let it all out before he explained, "He wanted me to lie to you in hopes you'd lie to me. Like I said, it was just a dumb notion."

The prisoner still seemed to want to hear more about it. So Longarm said, expansively, "Oh, he told me to tell you that if you wanted to tell us who hired you to gun me the other day, and how come, I could just as easily take you to Fort Smith instead of Juarez, hangings being conducted more scientific at Fort Smith. I told him to forget it."

The wheels clacked under them a while. Then Amarillo Jack asked how come it was such a dumb notion, adding, "I sure don't cotton to the notion of hanging Mex style. They don't drop you. They just throw the rope over a beam and hoist your feet barely off the ground so they can laugh at your gyrations, the sons of bitches. What would I have to say to get hung in Fort Smith, the right way?"

Longarm met the prisoner's eyes squarely as he told him, flat out, "Nothing you could tell me at this late date could buy you a Fort Smith hanging, Jack. I'd be proud to take down any lies you might want to hand me. I still have to deliver you to the rurales in the cold gray dawn. That's why I told Billy Vail I wouldn't do it. You'd have every right to call me a bastard if I played you so false, and I'd just wind up madder than I already am at you when I went back to Denver and couldn't prove your word one way or another. Anyone slick enough to hire another man to do his fighting for him would surely be slick enough to just deny the whole thing, even if you told the truth, which hardly seems likely."

Amarillo Jack started to say something, then he scowled across at Longarm and said, "You're trying to trick me, right?"

Longarm smiled thinly and said, "Sure I am. Don't the sky out there look swell, now? Looks like we're in for a mighty pretty sunset. I'd take a good look at it, if I was you. Of course, you never know. Mexico might want to hold a big trial before they dangle you. That could give you a few more sunsets to admire."

Then the porter knocked on the sliding door and Longarm slid it open with a boot heel to let their supper trays come in. He'd ordered steak and potatoes for both of them, seeing who had to pay for it, and told the porter they'd like more coffee, later. As the two of them grubbed, Amarillo Jack tried to bring up the Fort Smith offer again. Longarm said, "Eat your taters. Don't you know kids are going hungry in China this evening? I told you I can't take

74

you no place but Juarez. So why have more sins on your conscience? I know fibbing ain't the worse sin you've ever been guilty of, but it seems to me, this late in your career, you could use all the credit with Saint Pete that you can manage in such time as you have left."

"They promised they'd get me off if I got caught," Amarillo Jack said. "They never even sent me flowers in that hospital. If I had your word, Longarm—"

"Coffee's a mite weak," Longarm cut in, adding, "try to enjoy it anyway. Lord knows what they'll serve you in Juarez, if they offer you anything at all. I'd give you my word if I could, old son. I'd really like to know who's after me and that poor sweet little gal."

His prisoner blurted, "What gal?" Then he laughed, bitterly, and said, "No you don't. You don't get nothing until I get something."

Longarm agreed that sounded fair. They rode sort of tedious for a spell. Then the porter came for their trays and switched on the fancy new Edison lamp that was less trouble for a railroad to use than gas or oil lamps. That made it even harder to see outside as darkness fell. The train stopped to jerk water at a dinky prairie stop. Longarm wasn't expecting them to pick up any passengers. But they must have. For they'd barely started rolling again when the door slid open and a halfway pretty gal stuck her head in, looked blankly at them both, and said, "Oh, isn't this compartment B?"

Longarm told her she had the wrong end of the car and slid the door shut after her with his boot as she left, all flustered. Longarm said, "Lock must be busted. I'll mention it to that porter when he brings our coffee, later." Then he stood up and stretched, saying, "It sure cramps a man, sitting by the hour in one position. Why don't we swap seats and lean the other way a spell?"

Amarillo Jack didn't argue, albeit he needed help. Longarm made him comfortable with his cast across the gap closer to the door and adjusted his gun belt as he sat himself down, saying, "This feels better, for now. We'll swap again in, say, an hour. The idea is to keep your blood circulating. I get stiff on trains. Just as well we won't have to ride one all the way to Fort Smith."

Amarillo Jack asked hopefully, "Does that mean you've been dwelling on the notion?"

"Nope. I told you not to believe my boss. I have to turn you over in Juarez unless . . . Naw, forget it. That sounds too complicated."

Amarillo Jack said, "I don't mind complications. I reckon I'd be willing to turn myself inside out, right now, if that might change your mind about Juarez!"

Longarm got out two more smokes and took his own sweet time lighting up, as if he was considering hard, before he handed one to his prisoner, leaned back, and stated thoughtfully, "I just don't know. You could just be playing for time if I were to haul you all the way back to Denver to testify against the folk you were working for."

Amarillo Jack asked eagerly, "Could you *do* that? *Would* you do that? I told you I don't owe nobody spit!"

Longarm shrugged and said, "I'm studying on it," as, under them, the train picked up full speed. Longarm let the engine moan at a grade crossing before he explained grudgingly, "If you fed us a pile of bull we'd wind up looking stupid and feeling mad as hell at you. You'd wind up bruised as well as dangling in Mexico. So study on that before you bear false witness just to go on living, in misery, a mite longer."

"I have. The trial has to take more'n a month, and do I play my own cards right, I might not even wind up hung at all. I was hired in El Paso, by another gentleman of fortune called Soldier. Don't know his last name, but he's a gun of some repute. Soldier told me on the way to Denver that you might be in the way of some big shot and that I was to get a thousand for doing you as I tried to. You was right about that old army pistol carrying high. Soldier gave it to me, the son of a bitch. How do you like it so far?"

Longarm shrugged and said, "Not much. Could you point out face-one if I bothered to haul you all the way home from, say, Santa Fe?"

Amarillo Jack never got to answer. For just then that damned door slid open and a cuss stepped in with a double ten-gauge to blow the prisoner's head to bloody hash!

By that time, of course, Longarm had drawn, fired, and dropped the shotgunner across Amarillo Jack's lap. Then he kicked the door shut again and said, conversationally, "I believe it was *me* you had in mind. I thought that gal you sent to scout how we was seated dressed sort of country for private compartments."

The man he'd shot in the side of the face rolled off to the floor, blowing bloody bubbles and making all sorts of odd noises. Longarm leaned forward to pat him down, removed a derringer from his vest and said, "Shame on you. Seeing I busted your jaw and cut your tongue half off with my own less hasty shooting, I know you can't answer me. So just stay put down there and first aid should arrive any day now."

He cranked open the window to toss the shotgun out. He looked the cheap derringer over and tossed that after it, saying, "It sure is crowded in here." Then he got a good grip on what was left of Amarillo Jack and rolled that over the sill as well, explaining to his live guest, "He's more use to the coyotes than to us, now, with all that blood seeping out of him."

The door slid open to admit a conductor with his own gun out. He knew Longarm of old and put his hogleg away, shutting the door for privacy as he bitched, "I knew you boarded with a prisoner, Deputy Long. But for God's sake, look what you've done to the company's upholstery!"

Longarm said soothingly, "That's how come I got him on the floor. Cold water with a little lemon juice ought to get that blood out, if you have someone start before it has time to set. I need one of your fine first-aid kits as well. I feel sure I can keep him from bleeding to death on your carpet if only you'd be kind enough to fetch me some cotton waste, gauze bandages and tape."

The conductor said that was no problem and added, "He's sure in piss-poor shape. If I were you I'd stick him in the hospital when we stop at Santa Fe."

Longarm nodded, but then he thought, smiled wolfishly, and decided, "Aw, he ought to last until your last stop at the Rio Grande, Gus. The rurales are waiting there for me to deliver a prisoner and I'd sure hate to disappoint them."

Gus said, "Well, he's your prisoner. But if you ask me, it sounds sort of inhuman. Look at the poor boy. His face is so swollen and powder-burned his own mother wouldn't recognize him, and you've made a poor mute of him as well!"

Longarm smiled fondly down at the wounded killer at their feet and said, "Oh, that's all right. The rurales only want to hang him. They don't want to *talk* to him."

As soon as the train crew had helped him tidy up, Longarm went hunting. He found the cheaply dressed gal dozing in her coach seat because it had taken some time to bandage up his newfound prisoner and leave him handcuffed to his seat and wearing the leg irons Billy Vail insisted on a transporting officer dragging along whether he used 'em or not. Longarm got out his wallet and held it so his badge and I.D. showed before he nudged the gal awake and softly told her, "You're under arrest, ma'am. Get up and come with me quiet, lest we disturb the other passengers."

She did no such thing. She stared up at him owl-eyed to protest, "I ain't done nothing!" So he put his wallet away and just hauled her to her feet and frog-marched her along the aisle as only one or two others noticed and seemed to find it amusing.

The gal got even more excited when Longarm shoved her into his compartment, shut the door, and swung her about to face it as he patted her down for weapons. She gasped, "That's a mighty fresh way to search a lady, sir!"

To which he could only reply, from sad experience, "That's likely why so many gals pack a derringer down there. Since you don't seem to be

79

armed, you can sit down, now. We got some things to discuss."

She sank weakly into the empty seat, staring thundergasted at the other prisoner as she asked, "What have you done to poor Mr. Smith?"

Longarm said, "He brung it on himself. The reason he looks so odd is that his mouth is filled with cotton waste and, as you can see, I had to tape the whole bottom of his face. He won't be in such bad shape as long as he doesn't catch a head cold in the near future. You say he told you his name was Smith, ma'am? I sure admire originality. Now, suppose you tell me how come you stuck your sweet head in here just before Mr. Smith came in a heap less polite."

She stared at the wounded man, who could only stare back with hate-filled eyes, as she told Longarm, "He gave me a whole dollar to do that. He approached me as I was getting on and said he had a delicate situation on his hands. He said he'd seen you getting on, you being the one with the mustache and brown suit, and that he was an old pal of yours but that you might be traveling with a lady and not wanting to be disturbed. He asked me to sneak a look-see and so I did. I told him you seemed to be with a gent as had a busted leg and he told me that was swell, handed me the dollar, and told me to forget all about it."

Longarm cocked an eyebrow and asked, "Ain't you leaving something out?"

So she thought and added, "Oh, yes, he did ask which of you was riding forward and which was riding backways. I thought that was a dumb question. But I told him. Am I really under arrest, sir? I didn't know you was a lawman and I'm just a poor country girl as never meant any harm."

Longarm asked where she meant to get off. When she said Santa Fe he got out a silver dollar, handed it to her, and said, "We ain't all that far from there, now. Buy yourself some ribbon bows with this and forget all about this misunderstanding."

She put the extra coin she could doubtless use away, but as he helped her to her feet again she asked, "Is Mr. Smith in serious trouble, sir?"

Longarm assured her, "Nothing he can't get out of, if he's half as smart and helpful as you, ma'am. You just run along now, hear?"

So she did. Longarm slid the door shut after her and sat down facing his captive. He'd been smart enough to seat "Smith" on the soggy side. He said, "Well, Soldier, you can still nod your head or shake it, if you've a mind to. So we have a few details to work out."

Longarm guessed, from the flicker in the other man's eyes at the mention of the one name Amarillo Jack had given him, that if he wasn't talking to the one and original Soldier the cuss had to at least know who Soldier might be. Longarm lit a smoke, saying, "I'm sorry I have to smoke alone, old son. What might the name Porter mean to you?"

Again those mean eyes flickered. But when Longarm asked if Porter had hired him, the wounded man's head didn't move. So Longarm said, "I don't think you understand this situation, yet. You robbed both me and Mexico of a prisoner just now. As we speak, a reception committee is anxiously awaiting the arrival of old Amarillo Jack in Ciudad Juarez, and they get to string up a gringo so seldom that I don't doubt they've sold tickets in advance and set up a refreshment stand. It ain't my fault you blew your old pal's face off, and anyone can see why I had to mess up your own."

Longarm blew a thoughtful smoke ring, let it hang a spell between his faint smile and the prisoner's hate-filled eyes, then nodded and said, "The two of you wasn't exactly twins, with your faces on. But a gringo is a gringo down Mexico way, and I'd just hate to disappoint all them folk. It'd be my word against yours if you could talk, which you can't. So I reckon you'll do well enough. Lord knows you deserve to hang for at least the murder you committed right in front of me this evening, and it ought to save the taxpayers on this side of the border a heap if we just let *Mexico* string you up."

He let that sink in. Then he said, "The mastermind as sent you to rescue Amarillo Jack or silence him forever must have been worried about us making a deal, and he was right. You got him just as the conversation was getting interesting." He went on to fill the helpless killer in on his earlier words with the murdered prisoner, gave him time to digest it, and added, "I suspect you're higher up the totem pole than old Jack might have been. I know you can't talk all that much, but we could still manage a game of questions and answers if you'd like to turn state's evidence."

The chained and gagged killer neither nodded nor shook his head. He looked more sleepy than interested. Losing that much blood could take a lot out of a man. So Longarm said, "Pay attention, damnit. You won't feel half as detached when I hand you over to the rurales in the morning. I hope you ain't been listening to gossip about my fundamental decency. I may not be as low down and dirty as most of the folk you associate with. But you would have killed me in that very seat if I'd been dumb enough to go on sitting there once I suspected I'd been scouted. So don't count on me holding tender feelings about you. When they told you I was as decent a cuss as the situation might call for, they must have told you I'm a man of my word. So the joke will be on you if you think I'm bluffing."

The other man's eyes closed and his bandaged chin slumped down to his chest. Longarm muttered, "This is a hell of a time for a gent in your position to fall asleep." Then, when nothing else happened and the clicking wheels under them began to lull Longarm past endurance, he sighed, stood up, took some haywire out of the possibles bag he'd boarded with, and wired the fool door securely before he sat back down, made himself as comfortable as anyone could on a Pullman seat, and put out his smoke to catch forty winks.

He caught more than forty. For it was starting to get light again outside when Longarm awoke with a start to see the other cuss looming over him, and kicked the rascal back down before he was awake enough to mutter, "Oh, sorry, I didn't notice you were trying to piss. Go ahead and finish. I won't kick you no more."

His prisoner had apparently lost interest in the open commode. His eyes were glaring again. So Longarm said, "I'm glad to see you so chipper now. I fear we'll be rolling into El Paso before breakfast time. But, what the hell, I don't see how you could eat anything if they served it."

He lit a morning smoke, grimaced, and said, "I'd rather have coffee right now. But we all have to get by as best we can. Have you been considering my offer, old son?"

There was no answer. Longarm stared out at the dry hills they were winding through now, and after they'd rolled another mile or more he tried, "Your devotion to a lost cause does you credit. I know who you're working for. I'd just like to be able to *prove* it. All you have to do is nod one time and I'll just have to haul you all the way back to Denver. You can give us the details once your busted-up mouth has been fixed. Just nod that you was sent after us by Sidney Porter or someone on his payroll and we'll just stay aboard when they turn this fool train around at the border."

The silent prisoner did no such thing. There was a funny expression in his beady eyes. Was it hope or amusement? Longarm decided to go with hope. He didn't see what the cuss could feel amused about. He tried, "Loyalty to a boss who considers you dirt is carrying loyalty to stupidity. I know you boys were hired out of the gutter by a man too proud to screw his help. You mean no more to him than the team as pulls his fancy carriage to his fine house up on Capitol Hill. It ain't as if he'll ever pay you another plugged nickel, even if he had any further use for you. Make it easier on yourself, you damned fool."

This time there was no doubt that the rascal was laughing, mean, with his eyes. Longarm shrugged and said, "Well, it's not for me to say whether you or Porter got on top. But have it your way if you love him all that much."

The trip was far from over. But as they rolled ever closer to the end of the line Longarm smoked silently and displayed no further interest, even though he was interested as hell. In his six or eight years packing a badge Longarm had questioned many a suspect, and so he'd noticed that when talking didn't seem to be getting him anywhere, the silent treatment might. Most folk tended to get sort of edgy when they were just stared at. Many a suspect had just had to break the silence in the past. The trouble with this one was that he couldn't, cuss his busted jaw.

But Longarm wasn't going to be the one to give in. So the next thing they knew the train was slowing to a crawl in the El Paso yards. Longarm rose, stretched, and unwired the door as he explained, conversationally, "In case you don't already know, you border badman, the railyards of El Paso form a sort of hourglass with the railyard of Juarez, with the skinny part a two-track span across the Rio Grande. My boss worked it out with Mexico for the rurales to take delivery on the bridge, both sides trusting one another so much. If it was up to me, I'd turn you over to the Juarez P.D. But the rurales enjoy international incidents and it *was* rurales you gunned in that cantina that time."

His prisoner made a muffled sound of protest. Longarm smiled thinly and said, "Sure you did, *Amarillo Jack*. You can grunt and groan at them all you like with that wad of cotton waste where your tongue used to wag. They'll naturally be expecting you to fuss a mite as they haul you to the fiesta they'll be throwing in your honor."

He dropped to one knee to remove the leg irons as he added, "I don't want to pay for these if they take you off my hands sudden. They cost way more than them handcuffs. We got some sort of tricky tracks to skip across, anyways."

He put the leg irons in his possibles bag, un-cuffed his captive from the seat, and stood him up to lock his wrists behind him as the train hissed to a final stop. Then he picked up the possibles, slid the door open a mite, and said, "We'd best let the other passengers get off. You're a sort of ominous sight. We don't want to get off on the platform side in any case."

In the time they had left Longarm tried, "That's assuming you don't want to go back to Denver, of course. No? Well, I don't enjoy your company all that much, either, you silent cuss."

A few long moments later the corridor outside was clear. So Longarm marched his substitute for Amarillo Jack back to the rear platform, opened the chain on the far side, and helped the now sort of wild-eyed rascal down the steps to the gritty gravel of the yards, warning, "Watch your step, old son. Aside from all these rails you could trip over, they switch cars unexpected in any railyard. The span across the river is this way. Let's go."

They started walking south through the confu-sion of switch points and boxcars all about. Long-arm was the only one who had a choice in the matter. Somewhere a puffer-billy switch engine was banging boxcars into one another. So that was what Longarm was keeping a wary eye out for when, just ahead, on his side of the infernal international bridge, he spied a quartet of gents in the ominous big sombreros of the rurales and muttered, "Shit. Those boys are so used to riding roughshod over anyone and everything that they don't worry about getting lost. I wish *I* felt as if I owned the whole world. I'd say this was about your last chance to save your neck, Soldier."

The man he was herding toward those hard-case Mex lawmen must have thought so, too, for he was suddenly running like hell with his bandaged head down and his hands cuffed behind him. Longarm drew without thinking, then he was running after the damned fool, shouting, "Cut that out, you asshole! There's no place to go, and if you make me run another step I'll slap you silly!"

Then his prisoner had whipped around the end of a chain of standing boxcars, right in the path of some others being backed by that switch engine, and it was surprising how loud a man could scream through cotton waste as he got chewed to death by steel-flanged wheels, rolling over him slow.

Longarm couldn't do a thing until the engine itself backed over the mangled remains, smearing them further along the track with its pilot. As he gingerly approached the big red smear he put his gun away and sighed aloud, "Jesus, the poor bastard must have really thought I meant to hand him over!"

The Mexicans must have thought so, too. As they joined him by the sort of spread-out body one asked, quietly, "How could an hombre run like that with a bullet in his leg? They told us to expect a prisoner who'd been shot in the leg, no?"

Longarm said, truthfully enough, "The gent I just got off with had been shot in the jaw. You could see for yourselves if only I could locate his head. Oh, yonder it is, by that switch signal."

The rurale nodded and said, "I see it. Something must have been lost in the translation. If this is what is left of Amarillo Jack, you must be the notorious *Brazo Largo*, no?"

"That'd be Longarm in my lingo," the American

lawman replied. "I like famous better than notorious as well. Notorious sounds sort of sinister, and I'm just a good old boy when you get to know me."

The English-speaking rurale smiled wolfishly and said, "Oh, we know you very well, Brazo Largo. Why don't we all go have a talk about your last visit to our country with the captain, eh?"

Longarm smiled back just as sweetly to reply, "We ain't in your country right now. If it's all the same with you boys, I'd like to keep it that way."

The grinning Mex insisted, *"Pero no, Yanqui.* We were sent to bring back a wanted criminal and, as you can surely see, the one here and there at our feet is no longer socially presentable. We shall explain this to our captain, of course. But he is liable to be most annoyed with us if we return *empty-handed.* So, as they say, when there are no bananas at the market, bring back such fruit as you can manage, eh?"

Longarm swung to face all four of them, cussing himself for having put his six-gun back in its holster. The rurales packed Colt .45s and were trained to use them pretty good. Longarm sighed and said, "Well, assuming we're all packing five in the wheel, I don't like these odds at all, muchachos. But it's only fair to warn you I don't aim to go with you alive."

The one who spoke English translated. The other three grinned like mean little kids. Their leader said, "That can no doubt be arranged."

Then another voice called out in English, "What's going on out here? What are you greasers doing in Texas and how come we see bits and pieces of what sure looks like one of our boys spread about so cruel?"

Longarm turned so he could face the Mexicans and the two Texas Rangers bearing down on them at the same time. He recognized one of the Rangers and, being a fair-minded man, had to grant that old Cactus Collins was mean enough to ride for El Presidente Diaz or Attilla the Hun. So he said, "Hold your fire, Cactus. These Mex gents and me were just discussing a case of pure suicide. Nobody killed the poor bastard. He ran in front of the back of a train."

Cactus Collins nodded and said, "So the switch engine crew just informed us. They said they'd have been more willing to stop had the yards not been so cluttered with infernal *rurales*."

Longarm said, "These boys are in Texas as guests of the U.S. Justice Department. They came over the line a mite to meet me here with these mangled remains, before they got mangled, of course. Mexico had dibs on him for a killing or more south of the border and, as you can plainly see, he must not have wanted to hang in either land."

The two Rangers exchanged thoughtful looks. Then Cactus Collins shrugged and said, "Well, it ain't often we get such a clear crack at the murderous sons of bitches. But seeing you vouch for 'em, Longarm, I reckon we'll have to let it slide, this time." Then he turned to scowl at the rurales and demand, "Well, are you boys fixing to scrape your want together in one of them big hats or what?"

The English-speaking rurale sighed and said, "Pero no. Since he is dead, my government is satisfied that justice has been done and Texas is most welcome to what is left of him."

Cactus Collins asked, in that case, what they were waiting for. The rurale leader nodded and said, "We were just about to leave." Then he shot Longarm a curious look and softly asked him, *"Por que, Brazo Largo?"*

To which Longarm replied with a shrug, *"Por nada,"* and got a mild surprise when the Mex held out his hand and, as they shook, said, "I am called Hernan Marin y Lopez. Feel free to mention me should ever the need arise. Do we understand one another, gringo?"

Longarm smiled and replied, "Go with God, you greaser." The four of them started walking for Mexico, not looking back.

Cactus Collins asked Longarm, "What was that all about?"

"I ain't sure. But I did want a look at a Mexican beef cannery as long as I was down here, and unless that boy was just funning, I just might get away with it."

Chapter 6

The D&RG agreed to clean up the mess for nothing if Longarm would attend to the paperwork. It didn't take all that long, seeing the late "Amarillo Jack" had met his death wearing federal handcuffs and had been considered a pest by Texas as well. A deputy forced to kill a prisoner he was transporting was forced by department rules to bear the expenses of the resultant funeral. But the cost of planting an ashcan half-filled with railroad ballast and ground meat in the local potter's field only came to fifteen dollars, with a psalm reading thrown in. The rascal he'd really caught had had more than that in his jeans, and Longarm was still ahead after he'd paid for a hearty meal and hired an Indian pony and a Mexican stock saddle at a livery handy to the official border crossing.

Longarm forded the Rio Grande, or Rio Bravo

as it was known farther south, at a less official point, downstream and screened by willows and ten-foot reeds. For entering Ciudad Juarez by all the picky rules could be a bother.

The Diaz dictatorship called its regular army *Los Federales* and its federal police *Rurales*, or Rurals. They combined the duties of American state rangers and federal marshals, enforcing some laws no American would have stood for, and so, in practice, tended to turn up most anyplace to vex folk. The sprawling brawling border town of Juarez naturally had its own more reasonable police force, which in the interests of the local chamber of commerce tended to protect a visiting gringo often as it might bust his head. So once Longarm had made his way to the center of town by way of some discreet byways, he recalled from earlier visits he only had to watch out for those big gray rurale sombreros and the fleet-footed street kids who'd steal anything they could lay hands on with as much enthusiasm and no more sense of guilt than a Cheyenne horse thief. Most of the poor folk in Juarez were nigh pure Indian to begin with, no matter how many religious medals they sported. Anyone with one provable drop of Spanish blood was naturally pure white. So only the full-blood Chihuahua owned up to being mestizos, or breeds.

Few of the older Mex folk in Juarez could be described as anything but friendly when approached by anyone as good-natured as Longarm. He liked most everything Mex but their government, and since they just hated it, he found it easy enough to get along with the general population. Almost all the folk who worked at the main marketplace spoke enough English to deal with out-of-town visitors.

But Longarm knew they were pleased by his own attempts at their own lingo. So he asked directions in the same and soon found himself reining in out front of a sprawling adobe complex with CARNE INTERNACIONAL painted in faded blue above the main entrance. He tethered his hired pony and went in to flash his badge and credentials at the pretty "mestiza" receptionist in the business office. She seemed mighty impressed and ran to fetch the plant manager. This gent turned out to be a jolly-looking fat boy in a meat cutter's smock, as Anglo as Longarm—albeit his Spanish might have been better when he told the gal to go play somewhere else before he switched to English and told Longarm, pleasantly but firmly, "That U.S. badge don't cut ice worth mention in these parts, Deputy Long."

Longarm nodded and said, "You're not about to get an argument from me on that point. You don't even have to talk to me if you don't want to. On the other hand, I understand you do sell canned beef to the U.S. government on occasion."

The American running the Mexican plant stared back at him sort of owl-eyed innocent to reply, "Not directly. Wholesalers in the States take some of our product, cheaper than they'll ever get it from Omaha or Chicago, and pass it on to anyone they like. We've nothing to hide that Uncle Sam could be at all interested in. I can show you around, if you like."

Longarm said he'd like that a heap. So the fat boy led him on a tour of the facilities, which might have been more disturbing to someone less familiar with the beef industry than Longarm.

That cynical French writer who'd allowed nobody who liked to eat sausages should ever watch

93

'em being made had no doubt been through a combined slaughterhouse and meat-packing plant at some time. Longarm found conditions in this one no worse than most, and there was likely no way to make 'em all that better. It was a simple fact of nature that no matter how you went about killing a cow, there was considerable bawling, bleeding, and shitting between beef on the hoof and food on the table. The workmen they passed in the noisy evilselling maze were mostly good-natured Mexicans who swapped jokes and lied about their love lives as they went on killing and carving up cows. The cement flooring was slick as ice because from time to time they hosed it down to keep the blood and crud from drying and setting. When the plant manager told him a second time to watch his step, Longarm allowed he was really more interested in corned beef. So the fat boy steered him into other parts, where a long line of women and girls were stuffing tin cans with meat a couple of men kept slicing off sides of corned beef and dumping on work tables for them. The plant manager patted a dangling slab still wet from the pickle vats as if it were a baby's behind and announced over the babble of the Mex gals, "We use nothing but top-grade lean for our export stock. You want to see where we age it in pickle brine?"

"Not hardly. You don't have to show me where these cans get soldered shut and pressure cooked, neither. Anyone can see you turn out a decent product, here. Would you happen to be canning any dog food, here, as well?"

The plant manager shot him a curious look and asked, "Dog food in *cans*? That's a new one on me. Who on earth would pay enough to serve their dog

94

its grub tin-plated? We do let a local Mex butcher carry off scraps and offal for next to nothing. Some of it might wind up fed to dogs. You'd be surprised what poor Mexicans make fair stew and soup out of. We get more for the leftover hides and tallow, though."

He picked up an empty can from one of the work places along the long table and held it out to Longarm, explaining, "These are rolled and plated in Monterrey. Cost us more than cans from Penn State by the time Ciudad Mejico gets its rake-off. We'd be loco en la cabeza filling 'em with anything cheaper than food fit for humans. I never heard of anyone canning food for *pets*."

Longarm explained, "Some society dudes back East make pets indeed of their livestock. I've seen canned dog food advertised in the *Denver Post* for a heap more than *I'd* want to spend on a dog, but still less than a quarter the price of corned beef canned for human consumption. Try her this way. If I wanted to just buy a mess of paper labels from you, wholesale, how much would you charge and would you recall such a transaction?"

The plant manager frowned dubiously and replied, "I'd surely recall it, which I don't. For why would anyone want just the labels without the canned contents?"

Longarm explained, "Might save a heap of shipping charges, paper being so light and handy to stick most anywhere. Anyone working here could likely get his or her hands on, say, a gross of gummed labels, packed neatly in a box from the printer, right?"

The plant manager shook his head and said, "Wrong. This plant might look sort of sloppy to you, but we tally what comes in and goes out neater than *that*, for God's sake. Printing would cost a lot less down here, too, if it wasn't taxed like everything but the infernal flies. I'll deny this if you ever repeat it, but the can and labels cost us almost as much as the beef we can 'em with. It's only the lower cost of good Mex beef that allows us to show a profit here. Anything manufactured is taxed to highway robbery. So we keep careful records on such overhead, and I'd know if a full dozen cans or even paper labels got lost, strayed, or stolen. I got carbons of our purchase orders out front, if you'd like to paw through 'em."

Longarm had a better idea. He said, "Setting aside printed paper to wrap around cans somewhere else would be easier for a gent working overtime in a *printing plant*. You do get your outside printing done local, I hope?"

The meat packer nodded and said, "Sure, less'n a mile from here. Let's go back out front and I'll be proud to give you one of their business cards."

They did and Longarm left with the name and address of a Juarez lithographer a city block from the main bullring. Longarm had once had a part in a fireworks display at that bullring, and he sure hoped the local police had calmed down a mite about that. He had to ride over that way, anyhow.

The old Spanish gent who ran off everything from corned beef labels to bullfight posters in the back, he said, was more coy about showing Longarm around. He said the way he got such bright colors not to bleed in the rain despite the awful paper he had to work with was a trade secret and that he wasn't impressed by Longarm's Yanqui badge enough to risk him being an industrial spy.

Longarm didn't press it. He said, in Spanish, that he only wanted to know how easy it might be for, say, a printer's devil with extra expenses to set aside a few hundred bitty labels now and again. The old man looked insulted and informed him that all the hired help out back were blood kin and hence no doubt honest. He added, "Even if one of poorer relations wanted to do such a thing, and I don't see why anyone would, I would notice the theft of the *paper* no matter what he printed on it when my back was turned. Meaning no disrespect to our no doubt well-meaning government, I know it must cost a lot to run our glorious republic, for it costs an extra centavo each time we use a full sheet, and I am not a rich man. I would notice at once if that much paper was missing from my modest stocks."

Longarm said he'd take the old man's word on that, since it would have been rude to call an elder a liar, and they shook on it. It was heating up outside by now. He knew that if he didn't get that iced cerveza he was hankering for before la siesta set in, he was unlikely to get one this side of late afternoon. So since his pony was already tethered in front of the printing plant on the shady side, he crossed the street afoot to grab a seat under the awning of a sidewalk cantina and order some cold suds. The pretty, barefoot waitress told him they'd be closing for siesta any minute, but that he was free to sit out front and drink cerveza in the sunshine if that was his pleasure and he wanted to pay in advance. So he said that sounded fair and ordered two schooners while he was at it.

She fetched them directly and dimpled down at him even nicer when he tipped her as well with a gringo nickel. Then she went off somewhere to lie down until siesta was over.

Longarm didn't care. Unlike some less used to Mex ways, Longarm understood some of the common-sense customs of Hispanic culture. It was just as hot, this time of the day, in Texas to the north. But Texans, for all their good points, clung to the business hours of the British Isles, even though anyone with a lick of sense could see how different the climate was in these parts. Hispanics had come from a warm climate to begin with, and so they'd just gone on acting sensible when they wound up in a climate even more severe. It wasn't true that they were lazy good-for-nothings who took long naps when they should have been working. The shops shutting down all around would be open again once it cooled off a mite, and they'd stay open way past sundown after even Billy Vail had called it a day up in Denver. If you studied Mex shopkeepers instead of cussing them, you'd see they stayed open twelve hours a day or longer. You only had to get used to the notion that you couldn't go shopping between, say, high noon and three or four. Shopping was a lot more comfortable after dark in summer, down here, anyway.

Longarm hadn't come to Juarez to buy cactus candy or one of them straw vaqueros on a straw pony. He figured he'd be back in Texas by the time the town woke up again. For he was running out of notions. Meanwhile it was fairly cool under this awning and the cerveza tasted swell. Mex beer was another thing outsiders who'd never tasted it were dubious about. Neither the early Spanish nor the Indians they'd taken over from had drunk beer worth mention. So the Mexican beer industry had been started by German immigrants who'd come over in the forties after troubles in the old countries had scattered Germans and Irish to hell and breakfast. The results had been a fine list of German lagers, served chilled, the way Hispanics liked anything but coffee. They even put ice in their oversweetened tea. Beer made more sense.

As he sat there sipping his, the sun was starting to get to the rump of his pony across the way. So he knew he'd have to be moving on directly. The trouble was that he was stuck for a more sensible place to go. What they'd told him at the meat-packing plant held together. The old printer across the way could be fibbing. He'd admitted he was just getting by. But the notion of buying just labels in Mexico to wrap about cans of dog food in Denver seemed a mite complicated when one studied on the profits. That meat packer's point about even canned dog food having to cost *something* was well taken. Nobody worked for free, since Lincoln had signed that famous proclamation, so it had to cost something to steam off dog food labels and repaper the cans as corned beef. Government contracts were supposed to go to the lowest bidder, but as the old Indian Ring of the Grant Administration had proven, Uncle Sam had been known to pay top dollar for many an item meant for Indian consumption. All it took was a government purchasing agent with a drinking problem or a mistress he couldn't afford on his official salary. There were dozens of ways for the bids of less greedy contractors to get lost in the paperwork. That made as much sense as suspicions about a criminal conspiracy involving hot water and glue in the dead of night. Few reservation wards could read and write to begin with. It would be just as easy to dole out cans of dog food and just fib about what might be inside.

Longarm put down his first empty schooner and picked up the second to mutter at it, "I could be making a slick chess game out of simple cheating, you know. I do that all the time. It's what I get for forgetting that half the crooks in this greedy world ain't half as slick as me. I'd likely starve to death as a crook. I ain't got the simple mind for it. Gents as study that much on not getting caught usually wind up doing things honest."

He didn't get to finish the second cerveza. The blue door of the cantina opened a crack and the waitress hissed out at him to join her inside. So he did. When he found himself alone with her in the gloom of the shut-down main room he smiled down at her politely and said, "I can see it sure feels cooler in here. But what about my caballo?"

She said, "Someone will take care of your mount, Brazo Largo. You are the one who may be in danger. Come with me, por favor."

He did no such thing. He cast a wary look at all four dark corners as he asked, "Who decided to dub me Brazo Largo, muchacha?"

To which she answered with a knowing smile, "You have been described among my people. I was not certain until a youth who'd been drinking inside viewed you through the shutters, said he was certain you were Brazo Largo, and left by way of the back door. That is the way we must *leave*, muy pronto. The one who recognized you is known to be a police informer when he is not just getting drunk."

Longarm muttered, "Ouch," and followed as she led the way back to the alley. But he got out his derringer to palm it while her back was turned to

100

him. For following pretty Mex gals into an alley was seldom the most wise move a gringo with boots worth killing him for could make, in Ciudad Juarez or any other border town, for that matter.

He still had his boots on when he found himself forted up pretty good with her at the far end of the alley. The dinky chamber they were in had 'dobe walls a yard thick where they rose from the floor of clean-swept but bare dirt floor. The beams above looked as solid. The stout oaken door was barred on the inside, now, and the only window was really a bunch of beer-bottle bottoms set in cement to cast interesting green and amber light inside, and no doubt make a hell of a racket should anyone try to open it from outside. The furnishings consisted of a couple of chests and a pile of bedding on the floor in one corner, save the inevitable cross hanging on one wall with a childishly whittled doll-like figure nailed to it. She said her friends called her Linda.

That was likely the simple truth. She was mighty pretty, and that was all Linda meant in Spanish. Nobody in the various rebel movements of Mexico used their right names if they could help it.

He didn't ask if she was a rebel, or why. He didn't have to. Old Diaz had taken over promising to do wonders, and some few Mexicans and a heap of gents in Washington felt he had. But most of the common folk of Mexico had been left out, or worse yet, taxed beyond endurance by a dictatorship that kept calling its fool self a progressive stable democracy. All the new railroads and factories were owned by foreign investors, attracted by cheap labor and tax breaks from their progressive pal, Diaz. He still had to tax *somebody*, and it was no doubt a pain in the ass to work for so little and pay taxes no American would have put up with. So the Mexicans didn't want to put up with them either. But every time someone protested in public, the rurales shot them. The results were a smoldering blanket of resentment that seemed sure to burst into flames any day now, if only the rival rebel factions could agree on anything but their hatred for the government. It was tough to get a good revolution going when everybody wanted to be a chief and nobody wanted to be an Indian.

Whatever rival faction Linda belonged to, she sat him on the bedding in the corner, sat down beside him, and said, "Forgive me. I was not expecting company. I have nothing for to serve you. I was told to keep you safe and comfortable as I could until la siesta is over. You would be a moving target outside with the streets so deserted. Your only hope is a dash for the border in the tricky light of sundown, with the streets crowded, eh?"

He nodded, reached absently for a smoke, discovered he'd run out of cheroots, and said, "I'm sure glad I got that drink-and-a-half down, at least. Where might my caballo be when it's safe to make a run for it, Linda?"

"In the stable across the alley," she said, "watered and fed with its saddle in place. I have an olla of water, if you get thirsty. Is *calor* in here, now, no?"

He allowed he'd spent many a lazy afternoon in cooler surroundings, and that he'd just get rid of his hat and coat if she didn't mind. She didn't. So he took off his vest as well and placed his gun rig, handy, atop his piled duds. He slipped the derringer down between the wall and bedding on his side

102

without drawing her attention to it. They made small talk for a spell, but they could both see it figured to be a long afternoon. He saw no need to tell her what he was doing in her country, and she told him even less about her plans to overthrow the current government. After they'd just been sitting there a spell she yawned and said, "If I did not have company, I would be stretched out here asleep. Is a much more comfortable way to spend la siesta."

He told her not to mind him and go right ahead. But she said she never slept with her duds on. He agreed that sounded sort of sweaty and suggested, "It's too bad we don't know one another better. I'd sure like to stretch out naked, too, and *quien sabe*, we might even wind up *sleeping*, in time."

She laughed in a sort of earthy way and said, "I have heard tales of the way el Brazo Largo behaves in bed. I confess I have often wondered if half the things some muchachas say about you could be true."

Longarm laughed back and allowed he was more than willing to show her. But she still put up the usual weak wiggles and faint protestations before he'd convinced her, in the end, that he was as marvelous a lover as she'd heard. She was sort of marvelous in her own right, once he'd gotten her out of that cotton blouse and simple skirt she'd started out with, wearing nothing under either. She sure looked swell, on top, with the green and amber beams from her improvised window painting her tawny young body with so many shifting patterns as she bobbed up and down like that. Like a lot of gals with Indian blood, Linda bobbed atop a man with her bare heels planted firmly under her firm rump and strong thighs so she could bob up and down and around in

103

a most delightful manner. She said he moved mighty fine when it was his turn on top again, although she did more than half the work as she kept time with his thrusts with her lively bounces. She was used to the firm floor under her, he could tell, as she bounced like a rubber ball in heat.

His only complaint, had he been rude or silly enough to complain about the way she was treating him, was that she acted too passionate to kill the tedious siesta time with spread-out fun. She went at it like a sweets-famished kid let loose in a candy shop, and between that and the afternoon heat, he was starting to feel the effects of the little sleep he'd managed the night before. So the next thing he knew they'd climaxed more times than he'd kept count of, and he noticed he seemed to be waking up on the rumpled bedding, alone.

He reached without thinking for the six-gun he'd left aboard his nearby duds, noticed that was missing as well, and propped himself up on an elbow to face the three men standing over him in the gathering dusk and mutter, "Buenos noches. I thought I heard a door open, just now."

The three Mexicans just stared down at him, like lined-up wooden Indians. One of them had Longarm's gun rig draped over an elbow. Their own guns were still holstered. That didn't mean much. Had they meant to just gun him they'd have done so when the perfidious Linda let them in. He didn't ask where she'd run off to. Right now he didn't care. He tried, "Might the title of El Gato mean anything to you muchachos?"

The one in the middle shrugged and said, "El Gato leads another faction, Brazo Largo. We are more interested in your friends who ride with Los

Rurales. The word on the street is that a rurale ser-geant called Hernan Marin y Lopez has put out word that you are not to be molested. We are most anxious to hear your answer to this charge, traitor!"

Longarm reached for his duds and proceeded to slip into them as he replied, soberly, "I fail to see how I could be a traitor to your *revolucion* even if I wanted to be. Do I look Mex? El Gato can tell you I've helped your cause more than I might have hurt it in the past. Old Hernan must have known that when he told his pals not to mess with me this trip."

The Mexican speaking for the trio said, "You *admit* you are friends with Los Rurales? You may as well say your prayers as you get ready to come out-side with us."

Longarm hauled on his boots, leaned back against the wall, and said, "Friends would be put-ting it way too strong. I let that one rurale live for the simple reason that I already had one body on my hands to explain in El Paso. He must have taken it more to heart than I did. That's all there was to it."

The rebel spokesman said, "It was more than enough if you had the chance to kill a rurale and did not take it. You are convicted by your own words, gringo. You will come with us, now. We promised the puta we would not kill you here in her quarters if she would be good enough to set you up for us."

Longarm sighed and said, "I can't say I feel any such obligation right now." Then he got to his feet, put on his hat, and shoved the derringer in their faces, adding, "I know this ain't much. But it's all she left me. I'd like my regular side arm back, now, por favor."

The one with the best view down the twin barrels

of the bitty derringer asked, more curious than scared, "Don't you know how to count to three, gringo?"

So Longarm answered, just as calmly, "I can count. I hope you can. We're all agreed I can only get two of you before I'm left in a hell of a fix. On the other hand, I'm *already* in a hell of a fix. So who'd like to go first?"

None of them seemed to want to. Longarm held out his free hand and said, "I'd like my gun rig back, now. I understand how you hombres feel about that. But as those rurales found out, earlier, I'm really a good-natured cuss when I'm allowed to be. You have my word I won't hurt any of you if only you'll be kind enough to give me my damned gun and get out of my damned way."

The one holding Longarm's gun rig sighed and handed it over without waiting to be told to. Longarm nodded, waved the three of them away from the door and backed out of it, covering them with his derringer. Once he was out in the alley he drew the .44-40, but, for some reason, none of them saw fit to follow after him. So he just strapped his gun rig back on and, seeing he'd paid a deposit on that livery mount and saddle in any case, he just helped himself to one of the three ponies tethered handy near Linda's little love nest, and rode off down the alley on it after turning the other two loose to run the other way. A gal who lied about police informers when she was out to do a poor man dirt would have lied just as much about everything else.

He heard them yelling behind him before he'd ridden far. He knew they expected him to streak for the border. So he cut the other way as soon as he was out of sight, circled to ride out into the corn-

106

fields around town for a time, then holed up in a clump of mesquite on the south side of town until it finished getting dark as hell. After that it was easy enough to cross the river way downstream, wondering why in thunder he'd ever been dumb enough to visit Mexico again in the first place. Billy Vail kept *telling* him that sooner or later he was surely going to get in trouble down Mexico way.

Chapter 7

That was the only thing Billy Vail gave him hell about when he got back to Denver the next afternoon. In the end Vail glanced at his banjo clock and decided, "Well, Mexico is content that old Amarillo Jack was brung to justice, even if you did deliver him sort of sloppy, and the less said about a hobo in a leg cast as must have fallen off a freight the better. It's a mite late in the day to put you back to work. So knock off early and be ready to run up to Broomfield and give Guilfoyle a hand with that fence war in the morning."

Longarm scowled in amazed annoyance and said, "Hell, I know those old boys up to Broomfield and they don't really mean it. I'm still working on the Porter case, Billy."

Vail shook his fat head and said, "No you ain't. Porter beat the charges, as everyone but you seems

108

to have noticed. Before you cloud up and rain to no avail, old son, I was really paying heed just now when you filled me in on your unauthorized side trip to Mexico. You risked your sweet ass for nothing. It don't matter whether the sneaky bastard did all them sneaky things with dog food or not. He's lost his government contract, so he can't do it again. Even if you could prove that's what he done, before, we can't put him on trial twice for the same infernal offense. So why try?"

Longarm insisted, "Sending killers after me and Aurora Stone is another charge entire. The gal could still be in mortal danger and I don't feel so safe myself. You'd have had to've been there to fully grasp how noisy a ten gauge is, going off in a railroad compartment, you complacent cuss."

Vail nodded sagely and said, "Both them gents are dead. If that second one was the one as hired Amarillo Jack, the chain back to Porter is broken and Porter has to know that. He'd be an asshole to start another, now that he's free and clear for as long as he keeps his nose clean. He can't get at you up in Broomfield no matter what."

Longarm insisted, "What about Aurora?"

So Vail, not knowing the scared witness was shacked up with his senior deputy, replied, "If anyone planned on harming her they'd have done so by now, while you was out of town. How many times do I have to tell you the case is *closed*?"

Longarm said, "It ain't. Miss Aurora is waiting for me as we speak in a cute little love nest I ain't sure I want you to know about. That don't make her safe, does it?"

Vail cocked an eyebrow at Longarm and growled, "No woman is safe around *you*, damn your horny hide!" Then he thought, nodded, and said, "All right. You're likely right about that fence war. I know both clans, too. But I want your word that if you can't come up with something you can damnit *prove* by the end of this very week, you'll get off my back about it. Put the fool gal on a train to either coast if she's still fretting. She'll never get a book-keeping job in these parts, whether she was telling the truth about her last boss or not, and we just can't guard every flighty woman who's worried about what might or might not be under her bed. Have you any notion just how many women, and men as well, complain to the law about plots against their very lives?"

Longarm got to his feet, saying, "What I found under Miss Aurora's bed looked real enough to me. I'd best go tell her I'm back. The poor little thing must be scared skinny by now."

As he left, Billy Vail called after him, "I'm sure you'll find some way to comfort her. I mean that about you having just a few more days, lover boy!"

Longarm lit one of the cheroots he'd picked up at the El Paso depot as he wandered down the marble hall. His boss might have given him even more hell had he said he wasn't going directly back to the Sepulvada place.

The perky blonde they called Bubbles, even to her face, came out from the stenographer's pool when she spotted him smiling in at her from the hall. She was smiling, too, but said, "I don't get off for another hour, Custis, and they're using that office we snuck into now and then, you fresh thing."

He said, "I'm on duty, too, honey. Worse yet, I won't get off when you do. But hold the sweet invite and we'll talk about it another time. Right now I have another favor to ask of you."

Bubbles said she was willing to try anything that didn't hurt. He'd already known that. He patted her friendly where he knew she liked it and said, "I need copies of some records you can get at easier than me, Bubbles."

He got out the dining-car menu he'd made notes on the back of, coming up from El Paso, and handed it to her. Bubbles scanned it, frowned, and said, "Gee, I don't know, Custis. I do very little typing for the federal purchasing office."

Longarm insisted, "They don't know that. They have to be more used to your pretty face than mine. What's to prevent you from just ducking in, after quitting time, and making a few notes in your swell shorthand?"

"Nothing, I suppose. But why can't you just *ask* them? Are you afraid they'll take a deputy marshal for a British spy or something?"

"Deputy marshals make crooks more nervous than a sweet, little court stenographer. Should anyone ask you what you might be after, just tell 'em we're tying up some loose ends to the Porter case. Only try not to have to. I'm not asking you to fib for me. I'd just like to have them figures sort of discreet."

She giggled and said she knew just what he meant. She'd laughed even louder the time that cleaning woman had almost walked in on them and he'd gotten rid of her by telling her he was questioning a shady lady in that empty office after hours.

Bubbles wasn't one to shake friendly with in parting. So he kissed her good, stole a feel, and headed out to deal with a gal built darker and more

111

refined. It didn't take him long to make it to Sepul-vada's. He found himself walking faster as he got closer. Linda had been brunette, but a lot darker skinned, and he was sore at her now, in any case.

But when he let himself in above the stable and called out to Aurora, there was no answer. A big gray cat stood up in Longarm's stomach and commenced to swish its bushy tail about as he quickly checked all four rooms to make sure she wasn't just funning him. Then he found the note she'd left on the drainboard by the sink. It said she'd gone to look into another job and not to worry about her after all.

He swore, balled it up, and threw it in the coal hod as he muttered, "Me worry? What in thunder could have gotten into the crazy little gal?"

Then he recovered the scrap of paper again, spread it flat to read the address of her new job more objectively, and hauled out his pocket watch to consult it before he muttered, "All right, if they don't do her in by quitting time they'll likely tail her home to do it *here*, cuss her sweet empty head!"

He knew where the place was. He didn't know *what* it was until he'd just about run all the way to Butchertown to stand panting, across the street, and read the sign above the door. It read, MINING HARDWARE AND PROVISIONS, H. H. HARRISON & SONS.

He knew the outfit, now that he studied on it. They'd been established out west as long as he had. He'd have likely heard about it by now if they'd ever crooked anyone serious.

The mystery was why in thunder Aurora had taken such a dumb chance. Porter's place was only a couple of streets over! He knew Aurora was a sort of independent woman. She'd been the one who'd wanted to get on top. She had said she was anxious to get back to work and that she feared she'd never find a bookkeeping job in the business, now. So, right, she'd heard of an opening and jumped at it. It was a free country.

Longarm hunkered in a door niche to light a fresh smoke as he considered her enthusiasm for her chosen career. Bookkeeping was likely more interesting when you knew what you were doing. He *had* asked the Mex kid to deliver the newspapers along with the other provisions. Having nothing better to read, she'd spied the job offer in the want ads and jumped at the chance, assuming she was over yonder instead of floating down the South Platte at the moment.

He shook out his match and was about to cross over and just *ask* when he saw Aurora come out the front door, arm-in-arm with a sissy dressed young dude he'd never seen before. Neither of them saw him. So he stayed put and, once they'd passed him, heading for downtown Denver, he followed, keeping to the far side of the street. They weren't acting as sneaky as he was. So tailing them was a snap.

But as Longarm and many another lawman had long since learned to their chagrin, tailing suspicious folk was a lot like guard duty. Nine or more times out of ten you were wasting your time, and this turned out to be one such time, as far as the fancy-dressed dude walking Aurora as far as the corner went. He just put her in a hack he'd hailed and turned back. He'd have bumped noses with Longarm if they'd been on the same side of the street.

But since Aurora was still acting mighty odd, Longarm strode faster, busted into a run when her hired ride disputed the next crossing with a brewery dray, and swung up into the hack beside her, asking, "Have you gone out of your pretty head entire?"

She gasped, threw her arms around him, and blurted, "Oh, darling, I've been so worried about you!"

He kissed her back. Most men would have, and their hackman didn't seem to mind. Then Longarm replied, "*You've* been worried about *me*? What in thunder are you doing in Butchertown in broad day?"

"Looking for a job," she said, "and I just got a fine one. I know you told me to wait until you got back, Custis. But I was going mad with cabin fever in those four bitty rooms and, well, you weren't planning on supporting me forever, were you?"

He repressed a shudder occasioned by that grim thought as he insisted, "Maybe not. But it could still be a long way from safe for you in any part of town, and the rascal you tried to send to prison is still in business just a few streets over. Did you give your current address to anyone at your new job?"

She shook her head and replied, "Of course not. A girl has her reputation to consider. As you'll see in just a minute, I told our driver to let me off in front of the Rex Hotel. I had to give *some* address when I applied for the job at Harrison's, and I recalled that I was paid up for the week at the hotel."

Longarm relaxed half a mite, looked back to see how many sinister characters might be following their slow hack, and when he didn't spot any, leaned back beside the pretty but dumb Aurora to say, "All right. Tell me about H. H. Harrison and Sons."

She said, "Mr. Horatio Harrison seems to be a nice old gent. That was one of his sons who put me in this hack just now. I haven't met the older one, yet. They hired me on the spot, at a higher salary, when I told them who I'd worked for before and why I couldn't ever work for him again. They said they'd always found Mr. Porter a shifty-eyed business rival and that they'd been following the case with interest. I knew them by reputation when I applied for the job, of course. I didn't just go rushing *blind* into anything. I've heard Sidney Porter say, more than once, that old Horatio Harrison was too fussy about the wares he vends for his own good and, oh, Custis, you'll never guess who my new boss is selling rations to now!"

Longarm sighed and said, "The government has to get its Indian and army grub off somebody. Don't you find it just a mite suspicious that they wanted to hire Porter's bookkeeper as well?"

She must not have. She stared at him blankly for a time as that sank in. Then she smiled, uncertainly, and told him, "It was an open want ad in the paper, and there were other girls applying ahead of me this morning. They interviewed all of us and I didn't think I'd get the job until they acted so pleased to learn I'd tried to put Sidney Porter out of business and still didn't like him at all. Then they put me right to work in the office and, guess what, I'm to get a full day's pay for my first day on the job!"

"Doing what?" asked Longarm.

"Filing and recording business transactions, of course. It's going to take me a few days to get caught up. Their old bookkeeper quit on them and left the books in a real mess just as things were picking up again this year. Hector, the one who walked me to this hack, showed me all about their warehouse and went over the books with me most

115

of the day. That's why I think it's awfully sweet of them to pay me for the full day. I was just beginning to get the hang of things at quitting time."

Longarm saw they'd made it to the Rex by now. He helped her out and paid the driver before he took Aurora's arm to haul her into the hotel dining room via the street entrance, saying, "If I was after you with a gun this would be about the last place *I'd* expect to find you as well. It's suppertime and we've got some nits to pick, honey."

As they took a table in the almost deserted dining room she went on gushing about her new employers. Longarm let her go on as he ordered steak and potatoes to go around. As the waitress left for the kitchen with their order he told her, "Never mind about Harrison and his fool sons. I can check them out easy enough, and I likely will when I get around to it. Like I keep trying to tell you, if only you'd listen, the sun ain't gone down yet and we're close to a mile from that hideout I went to so much trouble to find for a couple of moving targets."

She reached across the tablecloth to take his hand as she lowered her lashes and murmured, "I can't wait to get you home, either. But I'm glad we're eating out this evening. I don't think I'll be in the mood for cooking, afterwards."

He smiled back at her fondly and meant it when he said, "I'd feel a mite insulted if you did. I've missed you, too. But it's you and *other* gents I'm worried about."

She made a wry face and protested, "Silly, both of the Harrison sons are married men. Hector was polite and respectful when we were alone in the warehouse or office some of the time today."

Longarm shook his head and insisted, "I ain't

worried about who might or might not want to kiss you, damnit. The gents I'm worried about have tried to kill the both of us and, as far as I know, they ain't been caught yet."

She nodded soberly and said, "I know. Of course I'm worried about that, Custis. But life must go on, and even a snail has to come out from under its shell now and then if it wants to *get* anywhere in life. Weren't *you* planning on ever working again?"

He grimaced and said, "Not any more than I could help it if my boss wasn't such a fuss. That's not the same, Aurora. I pack seven rounds in two weapons and it's my job to tangle with the likes of Sid Porter and his boys. You've stuck your head out of your shell way too soon, you ambitious little snail."

The waitress brought their steak and potatoes. Longarm had forgotten how hungry he was until he dug in. Aurora picked at her own grub with less enthusiasm, saying, "I hope your other appetites will be as lusty, tonight, darling. As for my going to work in the morning, a girl has other needs, you know, and *you* weren't planning to support me in style for the rest of my life, were you?"

He managed not to strangle on a lump of steak, washed it down with coffee, and had to reply, "I couldn't afford to marry up with a woman on what Uncle Sam sees fit to pay me, the stingy cuss. I sure wish you gals could refrain from such hasty notions as long as most men manage. The question before the house is keeping you alive right now, not supporting you in your old age."

He ate some more as she mostly just sat there, looking a mite vexed for some reason. He finally sighed and said, "I hope they serve cheese with the pie, here. I reckon if I escorted you to work in the morning and picked you up at quitting time you'd be about as safe as you were when we were guarding you during the trial. If the Harrisons meant to murder you inside their warehouse they'd have likely done so by now. Lord knows you gave them a swell chance. You walked right into the lions' den like a lost little lamb and, lucky for you, the lions turned out to be as innocent. I shudder to think what could have happened to you if you'd guessed wrong while I was clean out of town."

She gulped and said, "Good heavens, you do make a girl feel sort of dumb, now that she's had a chance to think about it. But what's done is done, and I'd say Harrison and sons were more like friendly tabby cats than lions. What do you imagine they'll think when they see me coming to work and leaving in the company of such a handsome stranger, lover?"

He waved the waitress back to order them two slabs of apple pie with cheese. When Aurora said she didn't want dessert he told the waitress to bring both pies in any case. Then he turned back to Aurora to say, "You don't have to tell 'em anything they can hold against your reputation, honey. I'm too well known that close to the stockyards to pussy-foot about it in any case. They know you just appeared in court against a rival they don't admire either. We'll just tell 'em I'm still keeping an eye on you as a federal witness who could be in at least some danger."

He'd said that in hopes of pleasing her. But she naturally felt obliged to take things strange. She sniffed and said, "My, won't you have the best of all possible worlds. And just how long do you plan to

118

let me work by day and be your play-pretty by night, for free?"

The waitress brought the two dessert plates before he could reply. So he'd had time to consider his words by the time he told her, softly, "I had to pay Sepulvada more than they charge at Emma Gould's, and old Emma wouldn't make me pay in any case if *that* was all I had in mind. I'd feel dumb leaving the going rates on the bed table for you every morning. I'd as soon bed down in another room if you feel I'm just hiding out with you as an excuse to take unfair advantage of a lady."

She stared at him with that unreadable stare favored by women and house cats when considering whether to purr or scratch. Then she lowered her lashes and said, "I'm sorry, darling. That was stupid of me. You know I'd pour a bucket of water over you if you really managed to fall asleep in another bed. It's just that this whole business has me so confused. How long do you think we have to go on like this before things can get back to normal?"

He proceeded to demolish both desserts, but only consumed half the first one, in the end, as he pondered her question and wound up answering, "I don't know, and that has me mighty proddy as well. I can't do much about old Porter and his thugs right now. But I sure mean to settle his hash, one way or the other, starting in the cold gray dawn!"

Chapter 8

As a matter of fact, the sun rose pink in the clear
skies of high summer on the high plains and a bird
was tweeting pretty, outside, as he got back inside
Aurora to wake them both all the way. He'd been
right about her looking a lot different under him
than old Linda, even though they were both bru-
nettes down there.

She responded just as friendly and, afterwards,
served him bacon and eggs, with coffee better than
the mud they'd brewed at the Rex the night before.
She put on fresh underthings from her overnight
case, but bitched a mite about having to wear the
same dress to work, it being the only decent one she
had this side of payday. She bitched a mite more
when, after he'd seen her safe to Butchertown, he
insisted on walking her all the way inside. He assured her she didn't look as if she'd just gone dog

style, and that anyone who'd found out she'd gone back to work could be out to do her even dirtier, most anyplace. So she led him into the front office of H. H. Harrison & Sons and introduced him to that same younger son. He didn't seem to mind being called Hector as much as Longarm would have. He had a firm shake and didn't look as sissy, close up. Despite his townee suit, his face was tanned about as much as a man who worked outdoors on occasion was supposed to look, and his hand was a mite callused as well as grip-worthy. When Aurora explained why a U.S. deputy was escorting her to and from work, not looking at either of them, Hector nodded and said, "Makes sense. Sid Porter and I went to school together and I've never forgotten the time he put a snake in the teacher's desk. I mean, we all put snakes in Miss Whitehead's desk, now and again. She did scream comical. But this one Sid used was a full-grown prairie rattler. Come mighty close to killing the poor old woman, and she'd never tried to put him in prison. My dad could tell you more about Sid's dad. They came west together, and to be fair to old Sid, his dad was *worse*."

Longarm said he'd sure like to hear more. So as Aurora sat down at a desk, her new boss led Longarm back to a corner cubby, built so that the old cuss crawfished behind his own desk could stare out at the interior of his warehouse in case anyone took it in his or her head to steal a pick handle or a can of beans.

Old Horatio Harrison looked like an older and frailer version of his son. His shake was weak as hell. Once the introductions were out of the way, the patriarch of the tribe offered Longarm a cigar as

121

well as a seat across the desk from him. His son left to do something more important. As soon as they'd both lit up, the old man said, "I can tell you many a tale of that old polecat, Sid Porter, Senior. Have you ever had a brain-stroke, son?"

When Longarm just stared blankly back at him the old man said, "I didn't think you looked old enough. My doc says I might not have another as long as I keep more regular hours and don't get as excited as I used to. I hope he's right. I didn't even know I'd had the first one 'til I described my odd feelings to him. I had her right here, about April, I think."

Longarm blinked in surprise and asked, "Should you be working at all, so soon after a stroke attack, sir?"

The old man replied with a fatalistic shrug, "They clear up or kill you no matter where you might be at the time. May as well be doing something useful. I was mighty surprised to find out what a stroke felt like. I'd had no idea they was so sneaky. I'd always figured a stroke would feel like it sounds. I wasn't planning on *having* one, of course. Then, one morning as I was going over the books, I couldn't get my left eye to see straight, and when I closed it there was all these funny colors dancing about. Jaggedy lines, as if someone had tried to draw lightning bolts on a blackboard with colored chalk as glowed in the dark. I figured my eyes were just tired. I could still read as good with my right eye, only my right one put figures in the wrong place or blanked them out entire, as if they'd been erased. I didn't notice 'til I stopped to eat lunch that my left leg felt funny, too. It didn't hurt at all. It just felt as if I was wearing a hip boot when I rubbed it.

The doc said I was lucky. I could still move it good as ever. It just felt like the hide had been tanned to saddle leather. I walked on over to the doc's the next day when I noticed how one side of my mouth couldn't seem to taste cigar smoke. The doc said I was a damned fool, told me I was lucky I hadn't just dropped dead on the street, and shoved me in the hospital for close to a month. They didn't do nothing for me there but take my money. I got better all by myself. Doc says they work like that, now and again. He said some crud was blocking some of the blood to the right side of my brain, even though I told him over and over it was my *left* side acting up. Anyway, I can see as good with both eyes again, and the leg's come back to life along with my tongue. Ain't that a bitch?"

Longarm agreed it sure was and asked, "Might your rival, Sid Porter, have tried to take advantage of you whilst you were laid up like that, sir?"

The old man shook his head and said, "Hell, that sneaky kid was the least of my worries. He's never been half the crook his father was. A man could take him for honest if he didn't know the fruit don't fall all that far from the tree. I raised my own two sons to be just as slick at business, albeit one hell of a lot more honest. It ain't true that you can't make a profit without cheating folk, Deputy Long. In the end a man's rep can pay off better than the nickels and dimes you lose by treating your customers decent. My oldest boy, Homer, is up to the Arapaho Agency as we speak, taking care of business we took away from Sid Porter just by not acting as greedy."

Longarm nodded and said, "I heard Uncle Sam was sore at him, even if he did beat the charges some damned way. Might you be feeding Indians that corned beef Carne Internacional was supposed to be canning for 'em in the first place, sir?"

The old man shook his head and asked, "Whatever for? We've a local supplier who gives us as good a price for edible stuff as anyone in Mexico can offer, by the time you pay the freight. We was wondering about that, following the trial in the *Post*. It makes no sense to ship beef all that way to a cow town like this one. I used to argue about such matters with Sid Senior, before he made a play for my woman, and I never spoke to him again when he recovered. He was always coming up with some slick notion that sounded way more complicated and sneaky than good business."

Longarm told the old wholesaler of his suspicions about just saying dog food came from a respectable Mexican meat packer and pasting new labels on the results. The old man laughed and said, "That sure sounds like Sid Senior. It's sort of nice to know his boy takes after him. A lot of us used to screw the boy's mother in the old days. She was willing, and Lord knows he had it coming. I only done it, myself, whilst he was in the hospital after a grab at my own woman's drawers, you understand. She was sore at him, too. The muley son of a bitch just couldn't do things honest when honesty was the best policy. Some gents are like that, you know."

Longarm nodded wearily and said, "I've noticed. That's the main reason I pack a badge. Are you suggesting even a born crook would go to all the trouble of buying dog food and repapering it as something costing a mite more just for the sheer joy of pulling a fast one?"

Old Harrison nodded and said, "Anyone with a

lick of sense can see how that was risking dollars to grub for pennies. The boy inherited a good going business he could have just run right with high profits and few efforts on his part. Lord knows how his father survived the investigation of the Indian Ring when the Hayes Administration cleaned things up after the Custer confusion. But he did, and kept his contracts to feed Indians as well. I'd be lying if I didn't allow my boys and me made many an effort to take the business away from the Porters. But he had the inside track and could have kept it, had he not messed up and handed it to us on a silver platter. I wonder where he got that dog food to begin with. They don't can such scraps this side of Chicago, as far as I know, and, like I said, freight charges."

Longarm enjoyed a long drag on the expensive cigar as he mulled it all over. Then he nodded and said, "You're right. Some gents must get more than I do out of cheating for the sheer fun of it. I'm glad you told me I don't have to poke about here in Butchertown for a dog food cannery. Saves me time I can no doubt use, and I can see I'm taking up your time as well. But as long as I'm here you might be able to help me study on at least one more matter. Your youngest boy just told me Porter played unusually vicious schoolboy pranks on harmless women. Might you recall anything along them lines?"

The old man nodded and said, "Yep. Poor Miss Whitehead died of a stroke shortly after, as a matter of fact. Hers must have been worse'n mine. Poor old spinster gal was a natural victim for her pupils, seeing as she fussed at 'em a lot and suffered screaming fits when they got back at her. I'm proud to say Hector considered it unfair to stick a real rattlesnake in her drawer that time, though. A while later he gave the Porter boy a good licking for making a gal they both liked throw up. Hector allowed, and his mother and me agreed, that sliding a horny toad down the back of a young gal's dress just wasn't funny at all. But how come we're talking about long-ago schoolboy pranks, Deputy Long?"

Longarm said, "Someone tried to play a mighty unfunny prank on that somewhat older gal you just hired as a bookkeeper. I found it before it went off. Some mean little kids grow out of it. I fear I may be dealing with one who hasn't."

Back up at the Federal Building, Bubbles sneaked Longarm into an office that didn't seem to be in use at the moment to show him how much she'd done for him. She'd even transcribed her shorthand notes to neatly typed onionskins, bless her almost empty blond head, and seemed to feel he owed her a good screwing for being so nice to *him*.

But he just kissed her passionately and told her he'd have to take a rain check on further passion for now. To begin with, if there was one place he didn't want to be caught with his pants down, the chambers of a federal judge had to be it. As a rule Longarm made it a point not to mess with gals where he picked up his pay, and never would have started up with pretty little Bubbles to begin with if she hadn't sort of raped him by surprise that time. That got them to the main problem. There was no such thing as a quickie, once Bubbles had her duds off with a man at her mercy. So he knew that even if he hadn't been shacked up with another gal with her own considerable demands, there was just no way

126

of getting anything done once he let *this* one have her way with him. He'd never been able to bust free of those sweet octopus arms and legs of hers in less than an hour or more, even had he wanted to. Making love to Bubbles was sort of like eating peanuts. She always wanted just one more as well. So before he could lose his resolve he kissed her some more, told her he'd take her up on her kind offer the moment he was free to do so, and got the hell out of there before she could unbutton his fly any further.

He knew better than to carry the typed notes to his own office to read. Neither Henry nor Billy Vail were apt to try and seduce him. But he'd learned in the army that you never let them know where you were if you didn't want them to put you to work that didn't really need to be done.

So he wound up at a corner table in the nearby Parthenon Saloon with a schooner of needled beer as well as the papers spread in front of him.

As he sipped and scanned he saw he'd risked his virtue for little that he hadn't already found out, albeit with a mite more effort. The government purchasing office knew less than he did. Their job was just to study requests for supplies and such by other agencies and either approve 'em or allow they *had* enough paper clips or whatever for now. The Arapaho agent had filed a bitch saying Porter had sent them provisions that failed to meet the standards set in their contract with anyone. That had been just about the time Aurora had contacted the government about the odd way her boss had been doing business with the Arapaho. So while he could have used a few more facts, it all added up the way everyone but that fool judge and jury had seen things. He wondered why.

As he folded the onionskins and put them away in a side pocket he spied a familiar figure at the bar. So he rose, joined Crawford of the *Denver Post* by the free lunch, and said, "I'd have gotten to your office this afternoon in any case. What can you tell me about an Arapaho agent called Dickerson or a supply outfit answering to Harrison and so forth?"

The heavyset reporter in a loud checked suit thought about Longarm's question before he answered. That was why Longarm had chosen Crawford to ask. The newspaperman was an old-timer who knew where a lot of things he couldn't print might be buried in and about Denver. Crawford washed down the boiled egg he'd been gnawing on before he decided, "No news is bad news, but I call 'em as I see 'em, Longarm. I know both the gents of old. Dickerson's a retired army officer with a good rep. Replaced the agent the Indian Ring put in under Grant, just in time to save us from another Indian war, as the Arapaho tell it. Is he of all people under investigation?"

Longarm finished the last of his schooner, signaled the barkeep for two refills, and said, "Simmer down, news hound. I'll take your word on the agent. What about the new outfit that'll be feeding his Indians?"

Crawford said, "Old man Harrison came out here with a cart of gold pans and such when the place was still called Cherry Creek. Merchants have ever made more out of any gold rush than most mining men. He'd wed a young gal of poor but honest stock and they had some kids. We're talking twenty-odd years ago. So by now the kids would be growed. I'd starve to death if everyone in town behaved like that family. They're the sort of folk as get their names in the paper no more than three times. When they get born, when they get married, and when they die. Old Horatio Harrison ain't ever even been sued or vice versa. The miners swear by him. Didn't know he provisioned Indians as well."

Longarm asked about Porter to be told, "Now there's the sort of family business as keeps me in business. I can't say Junior has been sued over shoddy to undelivered goods as often as his old man used to be. But we both know he just got off lucky in federal court. Is that the case you're on, pard?"

Longarm sipped some suds and replied, "Not officially, so don't go printing anything about this conversation if you ever want a real tip from me again. If Porter has a lick of sense it's over. There's no way I can touch him unless he makes the next move. It all depends on how smart he really is. You'd think a crook's own crooked lawyers would tell him that."

Crawford shook his head and said, "Don't bother sniffing that tree, Longarm. I know the law firm Porter hired. Allowing for the simple fact that all lawyers are sons of bitches, they're about as ethical as any others I know of."

Longarm scowled and asked, "Then how did they get the rascal off if they're so damned honest?"

"Lack of evidence. I covered the trial. It was Porter's word against that of his lady bookkeeper. The Indians ate all the other evidence. So it boiled down to her swearing he fed 'em bran and dog food and him swearing he'd never do such a thing. No Indians appeared in court for either side. Dickerson appeared to say his wards had told him their grub had tasted funny. Not making a habit of consuming Indian rations himself, he had to allow under cross-examination that he just couldn't say what the stuff

129

might have tasted like, and that it was true nobody had died or even gotten sick on whatever it was."

Crawford washed down some more boiled egg with beer before he added, "Porter swore on the stand that his bookkeeper was out to do him dirty because he wouldn't leave his wife for her. Have you considered that he could have been telling the simple truth, just this once?"

Longarm nodded and said, "I read about Sampson in the Good Book. Leaving her motive up for grabs, I'd find it easier to buy her as a mere troublemaker if someone hadn't tried to kill her, and me, come to study on it. Have you ever heard tell of a hired gun called Soldier, last name unknown?"

Crawford stared soberly at him to say, "Sure I have. He's bad medicine. Soldier Brown got his unusual nickname serving time in our own state prison, talking all night about all the soldiering he'd done, even though the other cons knew he was a deserter. He's said to be dangerous to all concerned with a gun in his hands. I understand he works cheap, too."

Longarm smiled thinly and said, "Not no more. I suspect I got him the other night. But you can't print that, either, if you don't want me to deny it. I'm glad I bumped in to you, old son. It's good to hear I might have scraped the bottom of the barrel. A man would have to be out of his mind, total, to go looking for a new gun crew with the law watching him close as me, and a pissed-off prosecution might, whether we are or not. I understand he only tried to murder his teacher once, when he was a schoolboy."

They shook on it and parted friendly. Outside, Longarm had more places to go than any really sensible reason to go to any of them. He might have gone back to the office had not a kid in knee pants come up to him and handed him a note. The kid ran off before Longarm could ask who'd given it to him. Longarm shrugged and unfolded it. The message said that Aurora needed him, on the double, but asked him to meet her by the stockyards, at the north end, rather than the place she was working now. It never said why. He frowned thoughtfully, put the mysterious message in his coat pocket with the onionskins Bubbles had typed, and just started walking, humming the old tune that went, "Farther along we'll know more about it. Farther along we'll understand why."

The lean dark gent dressed cow but all in black must have considered his ambush a lot slicker than it was, judging from the way he was smiling to himself as he lurked in the doorway of a defunct and hence unoccupied feed store with a swell view of the stockyards across the way. The sheep pens up this way were deserted as well. So there'd be no eyes at all, human or otherwise, to view the results when Longarm showed up for his tryst with Miss Aurora Stone. Only that wasn't quite the way things worked out.

Longarm swore softly when his boot heel crunched on a rotten plank inside the empty building and the figure in the doorway whirled to see who it might be, saw who it was, and went for his six-gun. Longarm fired low on purpose and folded the rascal over his gun belt like a jackknife. Then he waded through his own blue haze of gunsmoke to kick the man he'd dropped further into the empty shop, saying, "That was dumb. I naturally had my own out before I tried the other entrance. You might not croak if we get you to a doc in time, amigo. But first we're going to have us a little talk, ain't we?"

The man moaning in a fetal position at Longarm's feet held his ruptured guts tight with both hands and sobbed, "You wasn't supposed to meet the lady in *here*, damnit!"

Longarm said, "I know. Fortunate for me I'd read her real handwriting earlier. Note didn't make much sense in any case. Why would anyone, but someone like you, want to meet me amid all this desolation? If I got your gall bladder or either of your kidneys, just now, we don't have much time to talk. They have to clean you out pronto if they mean to bother at all. You can commence by telling me who hired you and how come. I find it hard to believe you had it in for me on your own. I'd have never forgot a cuss as ugly as you if I'd ever brushed with him in the past."

The gut-shot man at his feet moaned, "I think I'm dying, you cruel-hearted cuss."

"I think you could be right. But it's worth a try." Then he kicked his victim's own gun into a dusty corner, kicked his victim just a mite more gently, and said, "Let's see if I can convince you of how much I already know. Sid Porter was standing trial for crooking Indians, and when he found out my office was fixing to guard the only witness against him, it made him edgy. Not because I might be one of the deputies posted to guard her, but because he'd heard I get along better than most with Arapaho and so, if I got interested in the case at all, I might just be able to dig up another witness or more against him. How do you like it so far?"

132

The wounded bushwhacker said he was damnit wasting time and that he was no-shit going to die if they didn't get him a doc.

Longarm shook his head and said, "You can't ask a man favors before he owes you. Soldier sent Amarillo Jack to shut me up and we know how that turned out. Soldier is dead, too, by the way. Was it him or you as planted that bomb under Miss Aurora's bed? And I swear I'll kick you in the head if you say you don't know who *she* is. Never sign a lady's name to a note if you don't want me to think you might know who she might be."

The downed gunslick didn't answer. Longarm said, "Never mind all that. All I really need from you is a statement giving me the name of the bastard who sent you here today. It was Porter, no?"

This time, when the gent didn't answer, Longarm dropped to his haunches to feel the side of his throat with a free hand. Then he got back to his full height, muttering, "A lot of help *you* are, you sissy. I'd have never chanced aiming so low if I'd wanted you to die without making a statement I could use before a judge and jury!"

Somewhere outside, a police whistle was chirping. So Longarm reloaded, put away his gun, and stepped out into the bright sunlight as a worried-looking copper-badge came around the corner. They'd met before. So Longarm said, "That was my gun you just heard, Swensen. I got a suspect inside I'd like you to take a look at."

The copper-badge followed Longarm inside, whistled softly at the results of that one shot he'd heard in the distance, and opined, "The only thing I suspect this gent of is sudden death. You must be as good as they say, Longarm. That old boy was murder on the hoof!"

Longarm agreed, "He must have thought so, waiting for me here alone. You knew him, Swensen?"

The blue-uniformed Swensen answered, "Not to drink with. They sent us pictures along with his yellow sheets. He was known in life as Speedy Sullivan. Texas breed, noted for his quick draw and disregard for human life. There's a heap of money on this one, Longarm. He was wanted lots of places for lots of mean things. I'm sure glad it was you he run into on my beat!"

Longarm nodded down at the cadaver and said, "Me, too. Had he got you I'd have never guessed what he was doing in town. So let's study on that, old son. You local boys are allowed to put in for bounty money. My boss frowns on it. So all the tedious paperwork would just be an unprofitable chore for me and, to tell the truth, I'd like to move in mysterious ways for a change and, if we sort of change the story a harmless mite—"

Swensen cut in with, "I don't know, Longarm. I'd have to tell my sergeant, at least." So Longarm assured him he knew Sergeant Nolan even better, and in the end the young copper-badge allowed he sure could use the bounty and that it would be a shame to let it go to waste. They shook on it over the dead killer and Swensen said he'd take care of things, here, asking, "Are you sure I can't do anything else for you, pard?"

Longarm said, "A dying man's statement to a peace officer has been known to hold up in court, but the son of a bitch died on me before I could get one out of him. I'd best see if he had any other names and addresses on him, as long as I'm here."

But that didn't work, either. The only item of interest in the dead man's pockets was a railroad ticket stub. They'd both already known he was wanted in Texas. Longarm put the stub away, saying, "They might be able to give me the date of purchase at the Union Depot. If he just got here, it means someone is still in the market for hired guns. If he's been here all the while it won't mean anything I don't already know. It's been nice talking to you, Swensen."

The Union Depot was a short walk off. A ticket agent Longarm knew there was willing to check the number on the ticket stub, but it took nigh half an hour and didn't really help. The ticket had been purchased in El Paso about the time Soldier would have been recruiting Amarillo Jack as well. So Longarm was right back where he started, save the chance to pick up more cheroots at the depot newsstand, and still being alive, of course. As he lit one by the Wynkoop Street entrance he muttered, "It's my own fault for busting Soldier's jaw like that. With him gone the chain's broken, even if I do know where it leads."

Chapter 9

That evening Longarm waited until he had Aurora
calmed down and content with a good supper and
some of him inside her before he told her, gently,
about the sneaky note she'd never written him. She
shuddered her naked shoulders in his naked arms as
he finished, and said, "Oh, my God! That's awful!
Whatever are we to do now, darling? I was so sure
Mr. Porter had forgotten all about me!"

He patted her shoulder soothingly and said, "He
could hardly be expected to forget you, but he sure
should have dropped it by now. I'm surprised he let
his old teacher die a natural death in the end. I
reckon as long as he keeps proving he's just crazy-
mean, *I'm* going to have to prove it. He's commenc-
ing to strike me as a danger to the whole
community."

She snuggled closer to ask, "But how, Custis?

He's slick as well as scary. If you accuse him, he'll just grin at you with those beady little eyes daring you to prove he's ever whistled at a pretty ankle."

Longarm said, "I noticed. He beat you in court by insisting it was just your word against his. What we need is more witnesses. When you were keeping his books, did you ever notice anything aside from bad flour and bad meat he wanted to feed Indians?"

She thought before she said, "Well, there were some fishy figures about blankets. He billed them as wool, even though the invoices said they were cotton flannel. But the prosecution men told me not to make it sound too complicated for the jury and just stick to the really vile stuff about the dog food. Does it matter, darling?"

He kissed the part of her hair and said, "It might. Depends on whether they want to haul him in on yet another charge. They can't try him twice on those first charges, but any prosecutor worth his salt can get an Indian issued a bad blanket to bitch about bad food as well in front of a new jury. Porter's lawyers will object and the judge will have to sustain them. But the jurors will still have heard what a bastard Porter is. So I'll tell you what we'd best do."

He got a firmer grip on her and said, "You can't go to work in the morning. I'll drop by to tell 'em why you can't, and they won't fire you if it's in the interest of putting a rival out of business for keeps."

He'd been right about getting a good hold on her, first. She tried to sit up, demanding, "Why can't I go to work? My new job is interesting and I thought we'd settled that!"

He kissed her some more and soothed, "We have. You got the job. Now we just have to keep you alive until payday. I got to ride up to the Arapaho agency in the foothills. You got to stay here, safe, 'til I get back. It won't take me more than one day, and nobody else knows where to find you whilst I'm in no position to guard you, see?"

She didn't like it much, but she agreed in the end, after he'd argued almost as much as he'd made love to her. She fussed again in the morning. But once he'd made her so late with early-morning slap-and-tickle that she'd have had a time explaining, anyway, she agreed to stay holed up, just this one day. So he kissed her to seal the bargain and lit out for his own nearby rooming house to gather his McClellan and Winchester. He put both aboard one of old Sepulvada's ponies for hire and made up the lost time by riding it into town.

Old man Harrison was home in bed, feeling poorly. But he found both the sons that went with Harrison & Sons at work in the warehouse, and neither seemed to get sore when he explained Aurora couldn't make it this morning. The older one, Homer, didn't even know her. He said it was jake with him if it was jake with old Hector. Homer Harrison was a tad shorter, despite being older, and dressed more cow. It was easy to see why Hector did most of the office chores while he got to ride around, tending to outside interests of the firm. They both wanted to know where Longarm was headed on that buckskin pony out front. So he said he was on his way to the Diamond K spread, south of town. He hated to lie outright to such nice young cusses, but the fewer who knew, the fewer he might have to consider if something went sour at the Arapaho Agency in the opposite direction.

The foothills of the Front Range began a dozen-odd miles west of Denver. They looked a lot closer. He had to ride even farther to get to the agency, north of Lookout Mountain. So it was more like noon by the time he drifted in, after circling some on the rolling prairie just to make sure he was riding alone out there.

The Arapaho Nation had been of two minds when the Lakota Confederacy had raised all that hell and Sitting Bull had sent out a general invite to all the plains nations to join the party. Many had followed their Cheyenne cousins north to Little Big Horn. So now they were reserved over by Fort Reno with other penitents. The ones still allowed to dwell near their old Colorado hunting grounds had picked the winning side and, seeing there were so few of them as well, got to live higher on the hog with only token supervision. Some got into Denver regular, even if they did wind up paying higher prices than the government-licensed trading post charged and didn't get anything free on allotment day if they didn't get home in time.

Indians could be smart as Mexicans about hot dry afternoons. So the agency looked deserted as Long-arm rode in across the parched grass from the northeast. There was no fence, of course. It was only back East that folk thought reservations were prison camps rather than a place of refuge for Indian who couldn't or wouldn't support themselves. The Stars and Stripes drooped listlessly from the lodgepole pine flagstaff marking the center of creation. Around it clustered the main government issue buildings of whitewashed frame while, farther out and lined up less neatly, each Arapaho family had its own glorified doghouse. Indians could get whitewash, free, if they wanted to live in dinky white houses. But Plains Indians didn't. White was one medicine color of Death, black being the other, and they liked the sun-silvered gray of unpainted lumber just fine. Some few had trimmed their doors and window frames with green, or used green paint to draw stick figures and medicine signs on the otherwise bare walls. Green was a fine medicine color, to hear Arapaho tell it. The whole layout smelled odd to a white man for at least the first few sniffs. It wasn't true that Indians stunk *worse* than white settlers. Everybody stunk when they were living low on the financial totem pole. Nobody could stink worse than trash whites. Indians stuck in one place so they couldn't move away from untidy housekeeping just stunk *different*. Longarm got along well with Indians who weren't shooting at him, and tended to defend them against the mean-mouthing of less friendly whites. But he had learned, scouting for the army that time, that you really could detect an Indian camp by its odor just in time to have second thoughts about topping that next rise during times of trouble. Aside from the usual reek of smoke and pony shit you sniffed everywhere human beings might be, Indians left an aftertaste of their own in the air. Longarm had long since decided it had to be the food they ate and the way their women washed their duds with sudsy weeds instead of store-bought soap, and hung 'em to dry over smoky fires instead of just letting 'em flap in the sunlight like white ladies did. Longarm had fond memories of many an Indian lady, but it took some getting used to with a gal who thought she'd smell sweeter once she'd sort of smoked herself like a ham over smoldering lovegrass, sage and such. He'd been told by them, more than once, that bay-rum aftershave smelled just awful to a gal who preferred her meat smoke-cured.

The bigger house the white agent lived in with his white wife just stunk like a well-kept farmhouse as Longarm tethered his pony out front and mounted the front steps. Before he could knock, Agent Dickerson popped open the screen door to invite him in and tell him they were all out back on the cooler north side. Longarm followed him through the nice little house—it reeked of lemon-oil furniture polish—and the agent introduced him to the lady of the house, who said he was just in time for coffee and cake on the shaded back porch. They struck him as a nice old couple most folk would like to have as neighbors. Dickerson was a tall gray man who still kept his spine stiff as the army must have told him to, a lot, in the beginning. Flora Dickerson was almost as gray on top but she'd kept her swell figure, and once he'd bit into her fine cooking, Longarm suspected old Dickerson had the best of both sides of the marriage net. Once they were all well provided and seated on the shady back porch, having talked about the unimportant matters country folk had to talk about before they got down to business, Longarm explained why he'd come all the way out here on such a hot day. Dickerson heard him out until they got to those shoddy blankets and he cut in with a sad sigh to say, "I fear you're barking up the wrong tree if you want to reopen the Porter case. As a prosecution witness, I was there when Miss Aurora brung up blankets brighter than warm. I was the one as told them to forget that, lest Porter's lawyers twist it into more confusion."

The agent washed down some of his wife's fine marble cake with her swell Arbuckle brew and explained, "We issue used army blankets and cast-off army duds to those Indians who need 'em more than they care about their appearances. Fancier duds, blankets, ribbon bows and such are *sold* to them, for allotment cash, at the trading post across the way. The government don't pay dime-one for the trader's wares. He pays us for his license to trade out here. I understand Porter did send a few dozen blankets out here once. The colors run out in the wash or, for that matter, in the rain. The trader gave back store credit to the Indians as felt they'd been cheated. They have a time understanding goods are to be sold as-is or that the buyer should beware. That's why we only let licensed traders deal with 'em. It cuts down on the army overhead in ways most can't imagine."

Longarm nodded and said, "I follow your drift. I can see how such nitpicking might have confused a jury of townsmen even more."

Dickerson nodded and said, "That's what I told the trader when he wanted to pile on charges of his own. How was I to know they'd let such a worthless cheat as Porter off scot-free? Don't you go mad-dogging over to the trading post in this heat if you want to talk to him about Porter's dumb business dealings. Everyone who saw you riding in will likely be here, directly, if they want to talk to you at all."

His wife got up, sighing, "Land sakes," and went inside to make more coffee and rustle up more pastry. Longarm said, "I know what you think about Porter. What can you tell me about his rivals, the Harrisons, no ladies being present?"

Dickerson chuckled and said, "Hell, I have nothing to say about old Horatio Harrison and his boys that I couldn't say as freely in front of a lady. Old Horatio's a hard bargainer. That would be how

142

Porter got the contract out here to begin with. Old Horatio don't give breaks to his dear old Uncle Sam for buying in quantity. He counts a hundred pennies to every dollar, and if you suggest you might be able to get a better price somewhere else, he just smiles and tells you it's a free country and that most general stores mark up fifty to a hundred percent more than he does, assuming they're at all honest."

Dickerson drained the last of his cup, set it aside, and went on to say, "Sid Porter has always talked more charming. Harrison seems tougher to do business with until you notice he delivers just what he told you he was going to deliver, for no more and no less. We made sure the last bidding on Indian rations was competitive, and to tell the truth I was pleased when old H.H. won the contract fair and square. He's no fun to dicker with, but I have yet to deal with a more honest old skinflint."

Longarm nodded and said, "I sort of liked him, too. But tell me, is the old man still in charge, total, after having himself that stroke this spring?"

Dickerson stared soberly into the distance, as old men tend to when considering inevitables, and said, "He's had two strokes, if only he'd own up to it. But his boys were raised by a mighty fine example. They work as a team to cover all the bets their father covered by himself in his salad days. Homer drums up business while Hector mostly tends to the warehouse details. It works out swell. You couldn't drive a wedge between them boys on prices with a nine-pound hammer. So each makes up a half or more of their shrewd old man. I ain't looking forward to old Horatio's funeral. It was mournful enough when his wife passed away two years ago. But I doubt it'll make any difference dealing with H. H. Harrison

143

and Sons. His boys would be fools to change things, and he raised 'em smart."

Then Dickerson turned from Longarm to wave a couple of old Arapaho gents the rest of the way in. He introduced them to Longarm as Calling Bird and Green Paint. He didn't have to explain, as they shook all around, that they were spokesmen for the two bands quartered at this agency. Mrs. Dickerson came out with a tray of pastry divided in two piles to suit racial notions of taste, and Longarm noticed she'd brought a sugar bowl filled with white flour for the Indians to put in their own coffee if they wanted to. Longarm liked her even better, now that he saw she was so smart about Indians as well as thoughtful to everyone.

They'd just started on her offering when, sure enough, a white man wearing a clean shirt and dusty overalls joined them to sit with the Indians on the steps. Longarm wasn't surprised when Dickerson introduced the other old gent as Trader Cohen.

As they were being served by Dickerson's sweet old woman, the agent brought his visitors up to date on the reason for Longarm's visit. All three of them seemed to want to say mean things about Porter at once, and Green Paint thought Homer Harrison was likely two-hearted as well. He said, "That white boy spends too much on his outfit for a serious person. Who ever heard of a real cowhand with a silver-mounted saddle?"

Longarm smiled and said, "He's not a cowhand. He's a townsman who gets to ride more than most, is all."

But Green Paint insisted, "Then why does he dress like a cowhand, if real cowhands dressed so fancy? He reminds me of one of those carvings you put of *us* in front of tobacco shops in the city. You are wearing a business suit over your boots and gun rig, Longarm. You still look more cow than that Harrison boy does."

Dickerson soothed, "The boy's duds are likely younger as well. Are you saying your people are sore about their new rations?"

Green Paint shrugged and said, "No. The new supplies taste like food is supposed to taste. I just don't like silver-mounted saddles and white hats that have never been rolled in the dust even once. I knew a young Arapaho like that, one time. He put coup feathers he'd never really earned in his scalp lock. He almost got me killed when we raided the Pawnee and he refused to fight like a man!"

The more sedate Calling Bird shook his head wearily to say, "My brother is fly buzzing about things that don't matter. We are never going to have another war with these people, as long as they don't make us cross with them, so why are we talking about whether the young man who sells provisions for us is a real man or not? My people and I are very cross about that one they call Porter. The government told us they were going to lock him up for us. But they didn't. They let him go. I have tried to understand the white man's justice. I don't think anyone really understands it." Then he stared soberly at Longarm to add, "Hear me, we know where the two-hearted Porter can be found in Denver. If some of us rode in one day to take care of him in our own simple way, do you think we might get in trouble?"

Longarm laughed at the picture and said, "I'd get in trouble, myself, were I to just go after the skunk as I'd like to. I have to get more proof that he's a skunk. That's why I'm here. I was hoping some of your people might have some of the dog food he sold you, left as solid evidence."

Green Paint blinked and said, "I don't remember any of it tasting like dog. It didn't taste like any meat we'd ever eaten. We ate it, of course. It wasn't that bad. I don't think there could be any left. It was delivered to us before the rites of Snow-All-Melted, when there is much eating and... never mind."

Trader Cohen shot an anxious glance at the agent in charge as he murmured, "What can I tell you? I sold 'em just a few jugs at cost and it was only cider as may have aged a mite in storage."

Dickerson said, "I didn't hear that. Just remember it's your hide, not mine, if anyone gets nasty drunk. I thought we were on the subject of dog food sold as corned beef. At the trial, the rascal told the jury Indians weren't used to corned beef and must have just thought it tasted odd."

Trader Cohen nodded and said, "He had me half convinced before I saw it on paper that he'd bid to deliver bully beef and sent something worse. I told him last winter that Arapaho learned about meat in cans from army rations and that the army field rations are bully beef, like the British feed their troops. He said even the soldiers bitched that bully beef had no taste worth mention, and that he could get better tasting corned beef cheaper."

Dickerson nodded and said, "I recall the conversation. I should have paid more attention. Lord knows I like corned beef better than bully beef. But, then, I was raised more Scotch-Irish than Arapaho."

Green Paint snapped, "We told you it tasted

funny. Now it is all eaten. So how is Longarm to prove there was anything at all in those cans?"

Longarm brightened and said, "I ain't got time to bring you boys up to date on chemistry labs. But there's more than one in Denver as may be able to assay an old tin can. What might you folk do with tin cans, once you're done with 'em?"

As it turned out, they used a lot for target practice. But with the help of some Arapaho kids who just loved to poke about in the agency garbage dump, even without the approval of their elders, Longarm rode out an hour or so later with some swell scientific specimens in his saddlebag. He knew it would take a scientist to tell him whether the now mighty sun-bleached labels had ever been switched. They looked to him like the ones he'd seen them gluing on similar albeit less rusty cans at the Carne Internacional plant in Juarez. He couldn't tell a tin can made in old Mexico from one made in Penn State. But he knew the Denver branch of the Bureau of Standards, near the federal mint, would likely be able to. The contents, or rather the dark dry crud still sticking to the cracks inside the empty cans, had lost any smell it had ever had and Longarm wasn't about to taste it. There was only an outside chance the food lab at the general hospital might be able to prove enough, one way or the other. Meat was meat, once it dried down to almost nothing. He meant to point out that real corned beef ought to leave traces of pickle-brine chemicals while dog food had corn meal in it. But even if they were willing to back their findings in court, could the government reopen the case on the same fool charges? One judge and jury had already allowed Porter hadn't made anyone sick, and they'd no doubt thought the red rascals were lucky to get *any-thing* to eat, free, at the taxpayers' expense. To make it stick, this time, Longarm knew he needed more than just those squashed empty cans. He had to show Porter had done, or ordered, something more serious.

Then, as he was topping a rise on the buckskin, some son of a bitch came close to skinning the nape of his neck with a high-powered round. Longarm had the bushwhacker's likely position as he rolled from the saddle, as if he'd been hit, casually taking his Winchester along with him as he landed in a clump of soap weed and rolled. Nobody who wasn't dressed in tin ever stayed *in* a clump of soap weed. It was called yucca, or Spanish bayonet, further south. Its stiff spines rose eighteen or so inches from the central soapy corns that gave the stuff its north-range name. Each needle-shaped frond ended in a needle-sharp tip that could put an eye out and didn't feel all that grand through the seat of one's pants. But it made fair cover on the rolling short-grass prairie, being about the only cover there was atop the rises. So Longarm levered a round into the chamber of his saddle gun, took off his Stetson, and raised his eyes as far as he dared to peer through the soap weeds he was prone behind.

His buckskin had paused to graze on the next rise south. Old Sepulvada trained his stock not to run far with reins dragging, bless his vaquero heart. Longarm couldn't see hide or hair of the bush-whacker's mount. Unless he was afoot, which hardly seemed likely, he'd hidden his own pony in a draw before creeping up atop a rise to lay in wait like a damned old spider. Longarm couldn't see him, but the odds were that he was down behind an even bigger clump of soap weed along this very rise. The shot had come from that direction and there wasn't any handier cover within rifle-shot range. Longarm threaded the barrel of his Winchester through the stiff soap weed between them, muttering, "Come out, come out, wherever you are. Can't you see you *killed* me, you sissy son of a bitch?"

The unseen other must not have been convinced by Longarm's dramatic fall from sight. For instead of exposing himself he fired once more from behind his own soap weeds and Longarm, repaying in kind, lobbed a round into the distant puff of blue smoke before rolling away from his own smoke and flattening out to await the results.

There weren't any. A million years later, after he'd stayed put so still and silent that a big prairie grasshopper had landed on his right sleeve, to chew brown tweed experimentally, Longarm scared the shit out of it by sidewinding back to his old position for another look-see. But there was nothing to see. If he hadn't hit the son of a bitch he'd surely put him in a meditative mood. So they were even, and Longarm swore softly but with considerable malice as he saw this was shaping up to be a sweat-out under a sweaty sun. He'd been in this situation before. So he knew the loser was usually the one who got fidgety first. He recalled the time he'd spent a day and a night like this, only to learn in the end that the Shoshone he'd swapped lead with had been dead long enough to start bloating. It worked out even worse when you moved in too soon. He could only hope his invisible enemy might not know as much about such matters.

The bastard must have, if he wasn't dead. Longarm lost track of the time, but the sun was a lot lower when he caught movement out of the corner of his left eye and turned his head just enough to spy a young Indian, dressed cow, sitting his own black pony over yonder by the riderless and grazing buckskin. Longarm said or did nothing as the Indian kid reached out to gather the reins of the pony he'd dismounted from, headfirst. The cuss seemed to be leading his mount Longarm's way. The Indian got much closer before he paused again to call out, "You, behind those soap weeds, are you hurt or am I in trouble?"

Longarm had already noticed the kid was unarmed. He called back, "Neither. I'm pinned down. Or at least I thought I was. In your recent travels, might you have noticed another gent in this ridiculous position by them soap weeds to my west?"

The Indian called back, "Nobody there right now. I did see a rider off to the west, over an hour ago. He was headed south, likely for Denver. I waved at him, but he never waved back. He seemed to be in a hurry."

Longarm got to his feet, banging dust out of his tweeds with the hat in his free hand as he said, "I missed him, then. That's my pony you're holding, if you don't mind."

The Indian kid handed him the reins and watched with interest as Longarm remounted and shoved the Winchester back in its boot. When Longarm started walking the buckskin toward that other clump of soap weed, the young Arapaho tagged along, saying, "I know who you are. You're the lawman they call Longarm. They say you have a good heart. Why would anyone want to gun you, here on Indian range?"

Longarm said he didn't know and explained his

reasons for being out here to begin with. The Indian said, "You might have said something Green Paint didn't like. He's always bitching about something." Then, as they rounded the other soap weeds he pointed down and said, "The grass is still flat here. Look, I see two spent rifle shells."

Longarm growled, "I got eyes. I make 'em .45-70 Army Issue."

The Indian said, "Maybe. The B.I.A. issues us those same old Springfield single shots, now that the soldiers don't want them anymore. They are good rifles. But slow for fighting a man with a Winchester. I think the one after you got worried about that and ran away. He must not have been Arapaho, after all."

Longarm said, "You already told me he was streaking for the Denver city limits. It's been nice talking to you, but I have to do some streaking myself if I mean to catch up with that trapdoor Springfield before he can get rid of it in town."

Chapter 10

Some lawmen as lofty badged as Longarm tended to look down on the hard-working peasants who kept law and order on foot in blue uniforms and dumb hats. But Longarm was nice to most everyone he didn't have a warrant on. So he was on howdy terms with most of the Denver P.D., and that saved him a needless ride out of the way when a copper-badge hailed him on the South Platte Bridge, late that afternoon, to say, "Howdy, Longarm. Where've you been? You missed all the excitement this afternoon."

Longarm reined in to reply, "Not all of it. What's up?"

"Big shoot-out in Butchertown. That federal witness gal you boys was guarding at the Rex wound up dead, along with old man Harrison, and Homer Harrison wound up in the hospital as well!"

Longarm's jaw dropped. Then he called Sid Porter something dreadful and would have heeled his pony into a flat run had not the copper-badge yelled, "Hold it! I just told you you'd *missed* it all! Old Porter's in the federal lockup, bent out of shape considerable. It was your sidekicks, Smiley and Dutch, as was sent to arrest him."

Longarm nodded soberly and said, "He must have come quiet as a church mouse, then. Billy Vail must have been sore as hell if he sent those two homicidal maniacs. I hope they left a few square inches for me to bruise. But right now I got to get to the folk I like better. You say Miss Aurora and the old man are dead? She damnit wasn't supposed to come into town before I got back!"

The copper-badge shrugged and said, "Well, she must have. For the way I hear it, she, the old man, and his son Homer was in the front office when two gun waddies busted in and commenced to shoot the place up. The only one left to talk about it is Homer. He thinks they was mostly after the gal. They only put one round in him, and the old man just had another stroke and went down otherwise unharmed. But the gal's in the city morgue with at least four rounds in her, last count."

Longarm swore again, asked which hospital they'd carried the sole survivor to, and rode the rest of the way into town at a dead run and to hell with the rush hour. He jumped a couple of wagon tongues and a sidewalk watering trough along the way before he slid his mount to a spark-shooting stop on the stone walk in front of the hospital and dropped off to take the steps two at a time. Inside, a startled nurse told him she'd be proud to show him

153

to Homer Harrison's bedside if only he'd stop cussing so loud. So he shut up and let her.

As they made it to the second-story wing of private rooms he saw he'd been even later getting there than that copper-badge had explained. A couple of fashionably dressed but chalk-faced women were seated on a hall bench facing the one survivor's door. His younger brother, Hector, was pacing up and down between the door and two wives as if he expected someone to come out and tell them it was a boy. Longarm shook with Hector and said, "I just got back to town. I'm really sorry about your father. I liked him and, if it's any comfort at all, I just spent part of the day talking to folks who knew him better and ought to miss him even more."

Hector Harrison nodded gravely and said, "It's my brother we're most worried about right now. Dad had lived out his time as the Good Book allows, and the doc had told us we could expect him to just drop most any time. But my brother in there ain't twenty-five yet and had a good life ahead of him before those bastards shot him down like a dog!"

"I know how you feel," Longarm said. "I still have to ask a heap of questions. Do you have any notion at all what Aurora Stone was doing at your warehouse this afternoon? She wasn't supposed to be this side of Cherry Creek, and unless she was mighty stupid, it must have been important."

The younger Harrison brother looked blank and replied, "You told us this morning not to expect her in today. Dad wasn't supposed to be there, either. But you know how muley *he* was. Homer was just minding the front office because someone has to, even on a slow day. I was uptown with my wife,

Miranda. She's the one there with the black straw hat. Lily May, Homer's wife, is the one with the cherries on her own hat."

Longarm nodded at the two wide-eyed gals but said to Hector, "In other words, you weren't there and, no offense, you can't tell me all that much. I'd best go in and have a word with your brother now."

But the nurse who'd shown him this far and no further said, "You can't go in yet, Deputy Long. The doctor is examining him." So Longarm asked if he was allowed to smoke and she told him he couldn't do that, either. She was a pretty little thing, for such a fusser.

A heap of paces later a fat old gent with a white smock over his gray wool suit came out to ignore Longarm and tell Hector, "Your brother seems to be out of danger, now. I'm sure we've saved his arm as well. But he really needs rest more than anyone fussing over him right now. So why don't you take the ladies home and come back tomorrow during regular visiting hours? By then he ought to be bright-eyed and bushy-tailed again and bored enough to enjoy conversation."

"I have to tell him our dad is dead," insisted Hector.

But the old doc soothed, "He knows. He was lucid when the police arrived, and gave a full statement before we had to knock him out to get at the bullet in his shoulder. There's nothing you can tell him that he doesn't already know, and he's already depressed enough."

So Hector commenced to gather up the gals as Longarm cut the doc off before he could get away and said, "There's thing *I* need to know, and I'm U.S. Deputy Custis Long, Doc."

The doctor started to shake his head, read the intent in Longarm's eyes, and shrugged to say, "Just for a moment, then. Nurse Healy, here, will stay with you to make sure you don't needlessly upset him."

Nurse Healy, as the perky little redhead seemed to be called, nodded at Longarm, pushed a shushing finger to her lips, and tiptoed in with Longarm in tow.

The private room was dimly lit, with the curtains drawn against the sunset. As if he'd read Longarm's mind, the young gent propped up in bed with his left arm taped across his chest asked if he could have some light in here. Nurse Healy lit a gas fixture on the wall to prove the walls were really rose instead of chocolate brown. Homer Harrison smiled weakly up at Longarm as he nodded and said, "I'm sorry about your girl. She'd just shown up when they came in after her. They must have followed her. I was just about to ask why she'd come to work, after all, when things got confusing as hell. I went for my gun. I never made it. Next thing I knew I was on the floor with some of the workers from out back splashing water in my fool face. Dad had dropped dead behind the table she used to keep our books on. I thought they'd shot him, too. But they tell me he must have been stroked to death by all the excitement. I could see right off that she'd been shot. There was blood all over. But what was she *doing* there, Longarm?"

"I don't see how she can tell us now," replied Longarm, tight-lipped. Then he said, "That can wait. She was obviously there, and I'd warned her not to be. Did you get a good look at the bastards who gunned you as well, Homer?"

156

The wounded man sighed and said, "I'm sure there were two of them. I'd have known them had I ever seen either before. They were both dressed cow, or stockyards, at least. I'm sure one had on denim jeans. After that it gets sort of fuzzy. I've been trying to remember them better. But it all happened so fast. The boys in the back say they heard a burst of rapid fire, come out front on the double, and that the sons of bitches were already long gone. Billy Dodsworth, a barrel roller with more nerve than brains, ran out in the street after them with no more than a pick handle. Lucky for him there was nobody in sight either way."

Longarm stared soberly down at the youth in bed to say, "If they'd been after you, or your father, they'd have put more rounds in you than the gal. I *told* her not to leave the place I had her holed up in. What about the books she was keeping for you? Are they still there?"

Young Harrison looked blank and said, "I reckon so. Why would anyone else want 'em? My brother, Hector, had just hired Miss Aurora. I doubt she could have made a dozen entries in our books before she was killed, and they were all matters of public record. Has someone accused *us* of crooking customers?"

Longarm assured him, "Your outfit has a fine rep. Aurora told me she was just getting the hang of your business ledgers. She said they'd been left a mite confusing by your last bookkeeper, though. What can you tell me about that?"

Homer shrugged the one shoulder he could still move and said, "Old Pop Wayne kept the books confused because he drank too much on the job to count proper on his fingers. My kid brother had a

157

public accountant go over the books when he had to fire the poor old cuss. By the time he hired Miss Aurora a few days later our books were in fair shape. I can't think of a thing anyone could find in our records that would be worth a killing."

Longarm grimaced and said, "I doubt that was what they were after. It was the books she'd kept for Sid Porter that inspired him to threaten her life."

The wounded patient sighed and said, "He must have meant it. But I understand he's been picked up for her killing, right?"

Longarm shook his head and replied, "For seventy-two hours, tops, if he survives the rough treatment Smiley and Dutch put him through. We can't hold him any longer on suspicion. We have to *prove* it. You just now said he wasn't one of the men who shot you and Aurora Stone. Do you really expect him to confess he sent them, now that they've gotten clean away?"

Homer Harrison nodded up at Nurse Healy to say, "I'd like to get dressed now, ma'am. Just let me get my gun and boots on, and I don't need no judge and jury. That skunk killed a mighty nice young gal and scared my dear old dad to death!"

Nurse Healy not only told him not to be silly, but moved over to the wardrobe to help herself to Harrison's pants and gun rig as well. Then, staring soberly at Longarm with Homer's six-gun draped over her arm, she told him firmly, "You're starting to upset the patient. Let's go."

Longarm protested, "I ain't asked him all the questions I meant to, yet."

But she just sniffed and said, "Ask somebody else, then. I mean it."

158

She sounded like she did. So Longarm told Harrison to try and get some sleep and followed the starchy little redhead into the now-empty hallway. She said, "I'm sorry. I'm just dying to know who killed that other girl, too. But even I could see you were just making him go over the same ground, and the boy is not at all well."

"I noticed," Longarm said. "How bad off is he really, as one professional to another?"

Nurse Healy said, professionally, "Gunshot wounds can be tricky, as I feel sure you must know. The doctors are more worried about the course of the bullet that struck him than where it wound up. It did *him* less damage, in the end, than it did Miss Stone on its way through *her*. He didn't lose much blood, and he's probably feeling strong as he says right now. But if that girl suffered a lung infection or even a bad summer cold—"

Longarm cut in with, "Glugh. I doubt she was a consumptive, but I get the picture. How do docs figure things like that out?"

"Powder burns," she said. "They were firing point-blank and Mr. Harrison wasn't the only one those warehousemen had to throw water on. The muzzle blasts set the poor girl's bodice on fire. His wound was left by a cooler bullet. Add it up."

Longarm did and asked, "Did you see the bodies as well as the kid in there, Nurse Healy?"

"I did. They brought them all here in the same ambulance for us to sort out. The old man and the young girl are in the hospital morgue downstairs if you'd like to see them as well."

He started to say he hadn't had supper yet. Then he nodded and said, "I'd better. Neither one of 'em were supposed to be in that office this afternoon.

159

And I was handed a note asking me to go some-where and get shot. I'd best go through their duds as long as I'm here."

Nurse Healy put Harrison's pants and gun in her office along the way to the basement morgue. Long-arm was led to suspect she had to be some sort of head nurse. She sure acted bossy enough.

When they got down to the clammy basement and she told a colored gent on duty to slide out numbers 16 and 17, Longarm saw both bodies were stark naked, save the tags wired to their toes. Old man Harrison just looked dead. They could no doubt fix poor Aurora up for an open-casket cere-mony as well, seeing the five, not four, bullet wounds were spread across her chest where they wouldn't show when the undertaker dressed her. Longarm swallowed the green taste inspired by the dirty crimson burn around the little blue hole above her right nipple and said, "Close range. Point-blank, in fact. I see neither has been autopsied yet."

Nurse Healy said, "They'll get around to it in the morning. Hardly any need to, of course. The old man had a history of cerebral strokes, even when he wasn't excited. The female victim was obviously shot five times through the upper torso with one or more guns throwing .44-40 ammunition."

Longarm winced and said, "I wish they'd shot her with something less popular. But how can you tell without— Oh, right, they dug one out of old Homer upstairs. The number makes me suspect one man did all the shooting. I pack five in the wheel myself."

She looked confused. So he explained, "A six-gun totes safer with the firing pin riding on an empty chamber."

So she nodded brightly and said, "I see. One did all the shooting while his friend covered for him, right?"

"That's the way things look. Where might the duds you took off these folk be, Nurse Healy?"

She said her pals called her Helen, and sent the attendant to fetch the duds. From the way he scooted, Longarm suspected he didn't get to call her Helen. He told her she could call him Custis as he wondered, idly, how bossy she might be off duty. She slid both bodies back out of sight so the brine pipes could keep them wholesome for the autopsy team. He could see she was at least as used to death as he was. He sort of had to admire a woman who was neither ugly nor sissy.

He'd just managed to tell her that, and gotten her all blushy in her stiff white linen, when the attendant came back with a pile of stuff aboard a pushcart. The male and female belongings were in two neatly folded piles, with the high-button shoes both had been wearing between them. A fat manila envelope rode atop old Horatio Harrison's clothing. The colored gent explained that they'd found no personal belongings when they'd undressed the dead lady.

Longarm looked at Aurora's outfit first. He saw she'd gone to her death wearing her only dress and clean underthings. That was to say they'd *been* clean until she shit herself on the floor with five bullets pushed through her. The bodice of her fancy dress was burned away in places. He could see where the mixture of blood and the water the warehousemen had dumped on her had run. She'd been lying face-up when they came to put out the fire on her chest. He grimaced as he refolded the now most unfashionable summer dress, saying, "She wouldn't have come into town without so much as a coin purse. You don't get to sip a soda or ride a streetcar free no matter how pretty you are."

Nurse Healy suggested, "One of those workmen might have been tempted by an obvious change purse, you know. The ambulance report says nothing that appeared at all related to either body was left behind."

"Warehousemen are likely as honest as ambulance teamsters, or vice versa. Let's see if the old man was robbed."

He hadn't been. There was forty-odd dollars in silver certificates in the old man's wallet, and some loose change rolled out when Longarm emptied the contents of the envelope atop his folded duds. He muttered, "I never suspected robbery was the motive."

There was a wicked old clasp knife, a key ring, a big red kerchief, and other such odds and ends. Longarm picked up a neatly folded legal document, removed the rubber band keeping it so neat, and unfolded it. A quick scan told him it was one of those invites the government purchasing office sends out so prospective bidders could tender their own secret offers to Uncle Sam. It was dated two days back, meaning it had probably arrived in last morning's mail. Longarm knew how long stuff lay around once someone like old Bubbles typed them up. Bubbles might very well have typed this very announcement. There was nothing sinister about it. The post engineer up at Fort Collins needed more of that white paint the army seemed to want to paint all the rocks it could get at with. Longarm explained to the two helpful hospital workers, "This explains what the old man was doing at the warehouse when his doc had told him to take it easy and his sons weren't expecting him to come in. The outfit must sell paint as well as other supplies and provisions. The morning mail arrives after business hours have started, if one knows his business. The old man saw it was a business offer, sent to the family home instead of to the firm's Butchertown address. If it was addressed by at least one sweet bubble-brain I know up to the Federal Building, that's no mystery. The old man just got excited and ran down to the office with this, hoping to have Miss Aurora enter a low bid for a heap of paint. He wouldn't have known she wasn't supposed to be there."

He started putting everything back in the envelope as he added, "It's a shame either of 'em were there. The poor old cuss must have got the last shock of his life. Watching a pretty gal and your own son wind up full of bullets could make many a healthier man feel wobbly-kneed."

He nodded his thanks to the colored gent and told the nurse, "I left a jaded pony out front. It's time I made sure it hasn't suffered a stroke of its own. I'd best lead it down the street as far as the Star Livery and have them rub it down and water it, at least. I may be right back with some tin cans. I meant to carry 'em to County General. But a hospital is a hospital, and you do have a lab here as could assay some dried-out whatever and tell me what it might have been."

Helen Healy said, "Of course. You'd be surprised what we have to slide under a microscope in the wee small hours." So he said he'd be back and she walked him to the front entrance anyway.

They shook on it and he went down the steps to find the buckskin trying to graze the water pump he'd tethered it to.

He untethered the reins and led the pony afoot to the watering trough they'd jumped on the far side of the avenue. As it tried to drown its fool self Longarm told it, "Seeing you're still so chipper, you can save me some walking before I stall you safe at the Star. I know you've had a long day. So have I. I'll tell 'em to throw in some oats later."

Then he mounted up and rode for Butchertown. It was a lot closer riding than walking. When he got to the Harrison warehouse he saw lights were on inside. It saved him picking the locks he might have had to.

Inside, he found young Hector Harrison standing behind a table, going over the company books. Harrison looked relieved when he saw it was Longarm. He said, "You made me proddy with those questions about Miss Stone's bookkeeping. So once I had our wives bedded down at the house, I came down here for a look-see. Everything seems to be in order. Like I said, the poor gal was only with us a short time."

"You'd know your books better than I would," Longarm said. "Is that a gun you're packing under your frock coat, Hector?"

Harrison nodded and replied, "Of course I'm packing a gun after dark in this part of town. Do I look stupid? I was all alone here until just now."

Longarm nodded and said, "I noticed. What make of six-gun might you fancy, old son?"

Harrison shot him a puzzled frown and said, "Harrington Richardson .38. I'd be proud to show it to you if I wasn't worried about your reaction to my going for it. Are you accusing me of gunning my own brother, for Christ's sake?"

Longarm smiled thinly and said, "It's been known to happen. But I just can't see your brother covering up for you if you had. There are limits to even family loyalty."

Longarm stared about idly as he explained, "I'm sorry I have to keep asking dumb questions. I have to write up fool reports in triplicate, and it's best to have all my facts and figures straight lest they make me go over it all again, in writing. You haven't come across a lady's pocketbook or change purse anywhere around here, have you?"

Young Harrison looked blank, then said, "Nope. Is that what you came here to look for?"

"I won't know what I'm looking for until I find it. Aurora Stone lit out for town against my orders, but you'd have thought she might have seen fit to pack along at least some loose change, a comb, a powder puff and such. Few gals leave home barehanded and destitute when they don't have to."

He explored about until, under a desk near the front window, he found a familiar overnight bag. He hauled it out, placed it atop the desk, and said, "Well, this ain't exactly a change purse. But I know for a fact it was Aurora's."

Young Harrison seemed sincerely puzzled as he asked, "What on earth would a lady's traveling bag be doing under that desk? It wasn't where she worked."

"Traveling, most likely." He opened the bag to see why it had felt so heavy. He searched through the duds and lady's notions neatly crammed into the bag as he added, "She must have been planning on going somewhere without even saying adios, let alone where or why. She'd informed me she was a free spirit as couldn't abide suspense. But I never expected her to just bolt without telling me."

Young Harrison said, "She must have planned on leaving us at short notice, too. Try her this way. She packed her bag to leave town and dropped by to ask for her wages. We didn't owe her all that much, but every little bit helps. She didn't know she'd been spotted leaving the place where you lawmen were guarding her, and they followed her to gun her the moment she was off the sunlit street. It all falls in place from there, right?"

Longarm pursed his lips and mused aloud, "I didn't know when I came by, earlier, that you meant to take the day off. You'd have been the one to pay her back wages, I assume?"

Young Harrison nodded but said, "As a rule. Of course, Dad or Homer could have opened the safe had she asked for her money."

Longarm asked if anyone had checked the office safe since the shooting. Hector snorted and said, "Surely you jest. I told you I came down here tonight to make sure we hadn't been diddled. The safe was the first place I looked. There's not a penny lost, strayed, or stolen. Do you want me to open up and show you?"

Longarm shook his head and said, "I wouldn't know how much was supposed to be in it in the first place. It's less work for both of us if I take your word on that."

Young Harrison raised an eyebrow to say, "Thank you, I think. I get the impression you suspect everyone you've talked to, so far."

"It goes with my job. You'd be surprised how innocent some folk I've met up with have behaved

166

toward me in my time. My job would be lots easier if wicked folk owned up to their misdeeds right off. But, then, they wouldn't be all that wicked if they felt compelled to act so decent, would they?"

He closed Aurora's overnight bag and said, "I got to impound this as evidence. Otherwise, I'll be running along now. I'll let myself out."

But young Harrison followed him to the door, saying, "You likely know what you're doing. But don't you already have Sid Porter under lock and key, and can't you only hang a son of a bitch like him one time?"

"I don't see how we can hang him once on such evidence as we have. With poor Aurora dead we can't even ask her to swear under oath that he threatened her virtue, let alone her life. He says he never."

Young Harrison growled, "You just leave me alone with him for five minutes and I'll be proud to beat a full confession out of him. He couldn't fight for shit when we were schoolkids together."

"Beating confessions out of a crook only works with a dumb crook. That's why I don't go in for such methods myself. As they discovered one time in Salem, you can get most folk to confess to flying about on broomsticks if you hit 'em a few good licks. But smart crooks know all they have to do is repudiate their confession in open court. There's just no way to smack 'em some more in front of a judge and jury. So I'd best get cracking if I mean to hang anybody. It ain't that I don't have it all figured, old son. I got just about all the pieces of the puzzle put together, now. The bitch is that I still can't *prove* a goddamned thing!"

Chapter 11

Longarm left the overnight bag with his saddle and bridle in the tack room of the Star Livery, and walked the short distance back to the hospital with the cans he'd salvaged earlier that day at the Arapaho Agency. It felt more like a million years. He hadn't had much sleep the night before, thanks to poor little Aurora. It reminded him of the night they'd buried Roping Sally, up Montana way. Life was short enough as it came with the Good Book. It sort of jolted a man when it turned out even shorter, and it was sort of spooky to think of a pretty gal he'd been in bed with the night before lying stiff and bare on a table in the dark.

As he approached the hospital steps a familiar figure was coming the other way on stumpier legs. As they met, Marshal Vail said, "There you are and where have you been? Every time they tell me you went one place you seem to go another. I need a deposition from you, even though Smiley and Dutch did get a full confession out of Sidney Porter. It was like we thought. The late Aurora Stone tried to put him in jail, he acted like a sore loser, and now he's in jail for keeps."

Longarm grinned at the picture and said, "Lord knows he had a few licks coming. They say he was even mean as a little kid. But I ain't done here yet, Billy."

He held up the tin cans and added, "A pretty gal inside says they might be able to tell us what was really in these cans marked corned beef. You're welcome to tag along if you like and watch me wrap this case up scientifically."

Billy Vail tagged along, but insisted as they went in that Longarm was just wasting time. He said, "We don't need to prove Porter was crooking the government. We got him on the murder of a federal witness, and that's a hanging offense for sure!"

Another nurse asked them what they wanted and told them not to talk so loud. Longarm explained he was looking for Nurse Healy. The older and uglier one said to come with her and keep it in mind that most of the patients were trying to sleep right now. They wound up in Helen Healy's office again. As she rose to greet them, Longarm waved a tin can at the gun rig she'd hung on a wall hook. He said, "That's Homer Harrison's six-gun, Billy."

Vail growled, "I see it. Colt .45. What about it?"

Longarm said to just keep that in mind. Then he held out the tin cans to Helen Healy and said they were what he'd told her he wanted assayed. She took them from him gingerly and led the both of them out in the hall and down the stairwell to the

169

basement again. They wound up in a small but apparently well-equipped lab where an old coot in a white smock and green eyeshade presided over mysterious tools of his trade. Once the introductions and explanations were out of the way, the old coot took charge of the cans and said Longarm's request sounded interesting. But as he dug into the crud on the bottom of one can with a pair of long-nosed tweezers, he asked how long it had been baking in the sun. When Longarm told him at least a few months the lab man winced and said, "Now it's really getting interesting. I can swear to animal protein, one way or the other, as soon as I have some in a test tube with proper reactant. Telling corned beef from, say, ground-up scraps of various critters is going to take me longer."

Longarm said they could wait. Then he turned to Vail and said, "Long as we're waiting, I may as well ask Homer Harrison, upstairs, some questions I didn't think of before. You coming, boss?"

Vail nodded grudgingly, but the nurse protested, "He can't be disturbed now. It's almost ten and his doctors have ordered bed rest, not late-night conversations, Custis."

"I don't mean to tell him bedtime stories. We're working on a killing and he was there."

So though she tagged along, clucking like a pretty red hen, she knew better than to try and stop them. So it only took a few minutes to bust in on the gunshot victim, and he didn't seem to mind. He was propped up awake, reading. As they entered he looked up, put the book aside, and said, "Howdy, I seem to have drunk all the water you left me before, and I sure feel thirsty, Nurse."

So Helen Healy said she'd fetch him some and

warned the two lawmen not to excite her patient before she got back. As she ducked out, the man in bed chuckled and said, "I reckon she means it's all right to excite me whilst she's watching. I sure would like to excite her, now that I'm feeling better. But I wouldn't want you watching. What can I do for you gents?"

Longarm said, "Well, as long as my boss is here to say I've done everything by the book, it's my duty to inform you that you are under arrest for the murder of Aurora Stone, and I'll just be a good sport about all the times you tried to have me murdered as well. You wouldn't have gone after me personal had not all the guns you'd hired been eliminated one way or another."

Billy Vail looked more astounded than the firm-jawed young gent in the bed. He just stared back poker-faced as he softly said, "You don't *look* drunk or crazy, but you have to be one or the other. They killed my father and damned near killed *me* as well, you asshole."

Longarm shook his head and said, "Your father got excited and suffered a fatal stroke. I was the one who put that round of .44-40 in you, earlier today. My Winchester and six-gun fire the same handy ammo. When I winged you out on the prairie you lit right out while I lay pinned for well over an hour like the fool I was. That gave you plenty of time to beat me back to town. You'd told your brother you'd be there all afternoon. You never expected to find your dad and that gal waiting in the office when you tottered in, meaning to patch yourself up in private. I can't say whether your dad was felled by that stroke at the sight of you wounded, or whether it happened when you emptied your six-gun into that sweet young thing at point-blank range. It don't matter. It's going to be tough enough on your otherwise decent family as it is."

The accused killer didn't answer. He just sat there staring friendly as a snake set to strike. It was Billy Vail who objected, "Hold on, Longarm. This gent was armed with a .45 you just showed me, remember?"

Longarm nodded and said, "That's why I asked you to remember. He was never struck by a round passing through her. When they autopsy her they'll surely find she was killed by a .45, not by a .44-40 round they dug out of this little shit. It might be interesting to impound that .45 down the hall and see whether it's loaded or not. He says he never fired it once. I don't see how he could have reloaded in the time he had to work with after emptying the wheel into her, do you?"

Vail stared down at the man under the sheets to softly say, "Unless that gun is loaded you're in deep shit, old son."

Homer Harrison must have been able to see that. He fired at them from under the sheets, doing the bedding more damage than he did either lawman before they'd both drawn and fired back at him more directly.

Nurse Healy dashed in from the hall with a pitcher of water, took one look at the smoldering sheets, and emptied the pitcher on what was left of old Homer, yelling. "Oh, good heavens, what have you done to my patient?"

Longarm hauled the soggy bedding down to expose the now wet derringer gripped in the dead man's soaked fist, saying, "He ain't anyone's patient, now. I'm sorry, Billy. I might have known such a sneaky cuss would take a back-up gun to bed with him."

The nurse felt the side of Harrison's neck, though anyone could see he'd been shot more than once in the chest, and sobbed, "Oh, Lord, I'd best go fetch the resident!" and tore out again.

As her heels clicked off down the hall, Vail stared soberly at Longarm to ask, "How come we just did that? I mean, I know why we had to shoot him. It was him or us. But how come it was him or us? I thought Sidney Porter was behind all this bullshit. What made you suspect this young cuss to begin with?"

"Nobody but Aurora Stone knew I was riding out to the Arapaho Agency today. I didn't even tell you. Homer also made the mistake of referring to her as my gal, even though I never kiss and tell. His own brother assumed I was only a deputy out to guard her as a witness. So Aurora couldn't have bragged at the office about her love life."

"You mean you was playing slap-and-tickle with a witness I only told you to guard?" Billy Vail cut in.

"There you go. If *you* didn't know it, how could anyone *else*, unless she told him that as well. I got suckered by a perfidious woman, boss."

Vail favored him with a shrewd look and said, "I doubt you found it all that painful. She was one good-looking whatever. But you'd best back up and start at the beginning. For you're still confusing the shit out of me. Why would even a crook gun a two-faced gal he was in cahoots with? Was he sore because she betrayed you to him, and just wound up getting gunshot for his pains?"

"I'm sure it was more serious than that," Longarm said. "Since you want the facts in order: Once upon a time, there were two rival wholesale outfits, with bad blood between them going all the way back to schoolyard fistfights. Everyone agrees Sid Porter was almost as unethical in business as his father had been. So let's agree with this dead cuss on that. His own father was upright and square. Old Horatio wouldn't have stood for his sons crooking even a crook. The youngest boy, who'll be running things now, never tried, even though it vexed the whole clan to see Sid Porter getting government contracts by bidding lower than more honest contractors could have. Homer, there, got out and about more. He heard what thin ice Porter was skating on and, as many a traveling salesman seems prone to, he flirted more than either his wife or his more proper old man would have considered at all proper. Somewhere along the line he got on sneaky-friendly terms with Aurora Stone. I'd like to think he was more interested in her keeping books for a hated rival than he was her more charming qualities. I'd like to think elections were run on the level, too. I found her a warm-natured little minx with round heels."

Vail cut in to ask if he was explaining a criminal conspiracy or bragging about his love life. So Longarm nodded and said, "It ain't important what other services she had to offer. What he used her most for was to frame Sid Porter and get his government business. She crooked Porter's books and carried them to Uncle Sam. Porter might have threatened her. Most men would have in his position. He had to know she was framing him. What sort of a crooked businessman would sell dog food to the B.I.A. and *write it down* in a business ledger? She used that against him as well, albeit I doubt she ever

174

expected the federal government to put a round-the-clock guard on her. It must have scared her as well as cramping her style considerable. She had a hell of a time staying in touch with the real crook she was working with. But she was able to contact him now and again, somehow. We'll never know if it was her grand notion or his to make sure a deputy who knew more than most about Indian Agency matters was kept out of the case. I'd say it was him. Not because she was at all fond of me when Amarillo Jack made the first try, but because he was the one with the money to fund all their bullshit."

Vail nodded and said, "He must not have wanted to pay *her* much. That accounts for the dynamite planted in her room at the Rex, right?"

Longarm shook his head morosely and said, "Wrong. *She* was the one who planted the bomb, making sure it wouldn't go off too soon. Nobody else could have done so half as easy, with us out to protect the poor little thing. She made sure the clock on her bed table wasn't ticking and, sure enough, I heard ticking anyway and played into her hands. If it hadn't been me, she'd have noticed her clock was stopped, herself, when they brought her back from the courthouse. Anyone asked to account for loud ticks when nothing was supposed to be ticking would have jumped to the same fool conclusions I did."

Vail said, "All right, she planted a bomb to make it look as if Porter was out to get her. Keep going, damnit."

"That wasn't the reason. She wanted to get out of that downtown hotel so she'd be free to get closer to this dead rascal and the *money* he owed her. I found she'd do a lot for pure pleasure, but she must have felt used and abused after Harrison got her to throw away her high-salary job and failed to come up with a better offer. Lest she starve total in the meantime, and because she was getting edgy as the plot kept getting thicker than she'd expected, she seduced me, and I, like the fool we all are when it comes to pretty women, fed her, hid her out, or at least kept a roof over her head whilst she worked to convince me how innocent of treachery she had to be."

Longarm paused for breath, glanced wistfully down at the water puddles on the floor, and got out a smoke as he said, "I swear I wasn't just fooled because she was a great lay, Billy. I'd read about what happened to old Sampson long before I met her. I considered what she might or might not be getting out of doing Porter dirty, as he told us. I just didn't see anything. She'd lost her job. She was too pretty and Porter was too ugly to buy his crap about her being a woman scorned. Anyone could see she was unemployed and low on money. It took me longer to notice meaner looking folk bumping noses with me where only you or she had any reason to expect me to be. I knew right off you don't set your own deputies up. But, just the same, I told her and only her I was riding out to the Indian Agency today. She *had* to be the one as told *this* dead bastard. Had not he known, he'd have never been laying for me. He'd known, earlier, that a note from my sweet Aurora might persuade me to meet someone else at the sheep pens, but since that shooting ain't ours, official, just take my word that she was two-facing me every chance she got."

Billy Vail growled, "Consider your word took. Get to the reason he wound up shooting her this afternoon. Was it some sort of lovers' quarrel in the end, you horny rascal?"

Longarm shook his head and said, "Nobody was ever in love with anybody. Don't we all tell sweet fibs when all we really want is a good time? I reckon she was getting sort of fond of me. I know I was mighty fond of her, and she never acted like she *hated* me. But I think what was getting to her most was that she'd never signed on as a hired killer. She'd just agreed to frame her old boss and leave town with a pat on the ass and a handsome bonus. Whilst I was down Mexico way, whether I figured to come back or not, she took the bull by the horns and marched into the Harrison office to apply for a job she knew was open, and that she could fill just fine. It was the old man and the innocent Hector as hired her. Old Homer, there, must have shit his britches when he came in from the field to see her sitting there as if butter wouldn't melt in her mouth. I'm sure the first time he got her off to one side he told her she was loco en la cabeza and risking everything. I can picture her, now, telling him all he had to do was give her her damned *money* and she'd be on her way."

Vail glanced at the dead youth on the soggy mattress as he asked, "Why didn't he just give it to her, then? He must have known she'd turn him in if he double-crossed her. She had him on attempted murder, and if he accused her of crooking Porter's books, guess who'd wind up feeding Arapaho again."

"Let's just leave the business in the right family on our official report, Billy. I'm telling you the whole tale so you won't fuss at me when I leave a few things out on paper. Everyone agrees the Harrisons, what's left of 'em, will do better by the Indians and taxpayers in the end. That was why this poor cuss found himself strapped for ready cash. Both his dad and younger brother were content with honest profits, and inclined to pinch pennies as a result. Trying to kill me off before things fell apart on him cost Harrison a bundle, even hiring bush-league assassins he shouldn't have. It's one thing to stall a woman you owe money to. It's another thing entire to stiff an armed and dangerous man who already thinks he's working cheap. In all modesty, nobody's about to go up against a gent with my rep unless he's paid cash in advance and, since I was so tedious to kill, he must have wound up laying out his bank account as well as his salary and expenses before he was forced to go after me personal. There was just no way he could have asked his honest family for more."

Vail grimaced and said, "That would have made old Horatio suffer a stroke even earlier. But hold on. What was he expecting to wind up with, in the end, from all this expensive bullshit with sneaky bookkeepers and hired guns?"

Longarm said flatly, "A prosperous if honest business, of course. I don't think either son really wanted their old man to kick the bucket. I wouldn't have, had he been my dad. But they both knew he was not long for this world and that Homer was the eldest son, who'd surely take over the family firm any minute. Dismiss the notion of crooked business from your mind, Billy. Even Homer was smart enough to see it was in his own best interests to just inherit a fine old Denver firm and go on running it the same way. That didn't help his financial bind in the meantime, of course. Hector told me, earlier tonight, that nobody had been in their office safe. I'd say that means he and the old man had a pretty good notion what was supposed to be in it. Homer, there, had to work with his own cash, exclusive, lest he blow the whole deal."

Before Vail could answer, Helen Healy came in with a young intern wearing a sleep-rumpled smock and a harried expression. He started going through the motions of examining the cadaver for signs of life, even as he muttered, "This one's deader than that old lady down the hall, and she passed away at sundown. I fear the death certificate is going to have to read trauma occasioned by gunshots, gents. Nurse Healy has already told me you were lawmen. Would you mind telling me why you blew such big holes in this patient's chest?"

Billy Vail said, "Line of duty. Never fire a derringer at an arresting officer unless you want him to fire back. My deputy, here, was just explaining how come we were arresting him. Get to the part about the shoot-out in the office, Longarm."

Longarm said, "Oh, that's a heap easier. Things started to fall in place fast after that. Earlier this morning I warned Miss Aurora not to go to work because I'd be out of town most of the day. I reckon I'd no sooner told them that at her office and rode out like a fool before she got word to this cuss. But I don't think she told him to set me up. I think she told him she wanted out, and that while I was off playing cowboys and Indians all day would be a swell time to scoot. I don't know if she showed up with her traveling bag packed or came back with it later. Dead men tell no tales, and it don't really matter. What matters is that he stalled her. He may have even told her she'd have nothing to worry about when I didn't come back to town this evening. It didn't work. I shot him instead. Meanwhile his old dad had shown up. He wasn't supposed to. We'll never know for certain whether he was alive when Harrison got back, packing my round in his shoulder, or whether she confronted him ugly as she waited for her big payoff with her bag packed to go under that desk. Either way, it must have gotten uglier when young Homer staggered in. Whether the old man was already dead on the floor or fell down when he heard the gal demanding her money, and no doubt saying why, Homer could see they were alone together for the moment, that he'd never have a better chance to account for stopping a bullet whilst his brother thought he'd been there all the time, and, like I said, he was short of cash and nobody likes to hear a woman screaming at him. So he just shot her down and lay down beside her to put on his act when the workers from out back dashed in to see what all the noise was about. She must have told him, earlier, that neither the workers nor his kid brother had been snooping about the office whilst he was out acting sneaky with me. What more do you need, Billy, chalk pictures on an infernal blackboard?"

Vail shook his pudgy head soberly and said, "No, it all hangs together, and his shooting at us through them sheets was as good as a signed confession. I'd say we were done here."

The hospital resident said, "Speak for yourselves. I'm going to want a morgue litter up here, Nurse. You'd best fetch some attendants with pine oil and mops as well."

She nodded, shot Longarm a dirty look, and ducked out. He turned to Vail and said, "We'd best get out of here. I just hate the smell of pine oil, boss."

Vail said he did too. As they were going down the stairs in step, reloading their side arms, Vail chuckled and said, "I reckon we sort of owe Sidney Porter an apology, should he ever wake up again. I *told* Smiley and Dutch to take it easy, damnit, but the silly son of a bitch did put up a fight when they came to arrest him. He must have meant it, after all, when he said they had no call to arrest him. We'd best go back to the office and do all the paperwork before we let him out. He's sure to yell for his lawyers, and it's always best to let them get to sleep, first."

But as they reached the main floor Longarm took Vail's arm to suggest, "We'd best pay a visit to the basement, as long as we're here. I left me some assay work in the lab."

Vail bitched about the delay, but tagged along. As they both entered the cramped quarters of the lab, the old coot wearing the eyeshade looked up from his microscope to say, "This has been fun. I thought you told me to look for corned beef or dog food, Deputy Long."

Longarm explained he'd figured it had to be one or the other, but the lab man shook his head and said, "Paper pulp or possibly wood flour. The fibers are quite distinctive. Birch or poplar if you want an educated guess. Once wood's been thoroughly ground and pressure cooked, it's hard to be certain."

The two lawmen exchanged glances. Then Vail snorted in disbelief and demanded, "Hold on. Are you trying to tell me an Arapaho would eat *wood*, like a durned *termite*?"

181

Longarm laughed and said, "They told me it tasted odd, boss."

The lab man said, "As well it might have. Wood pulp ground so fine can't hurt you much, even though you can't digest it and it just goes on through. I've heard of it being used to adulterate animal feed. Whoever canned it knew a thing or two about that subject. Since it hadn't gone through anyone's digestive system, the rest of the recipe was intact. I found traces of beef bullion, corn starch to give it a smoother body, and stronger beef pickle than you really need to corn beef. That's aside from salt, other seasonings and artificial coloring. Mostly madder red. You're not supposed to use that in food, but it does make wood pulp look a lot like, well, dog food, at least."

Both lawmen laughed like hell. Billy Vail said, "I'd say you just got two of my deputies off assault charges, Professor. We'll just let the cuss study on it until the swelling goes down a mite."

He turned to Longarm to ask, "Can you believe it? All the time Porter was swearing in court that his bookkeeper had framed him, he knew that. Had she but known he'd shipped even *worse* grub to the poor Indians— How in thunder could they have ever *eaten* it?"

Longarm said, "They were having a spring festival and likely got it down with hard cider, boss. It's a pure shame little old Aurora and the cuss we shot upstairs went to all that trouble when all the time, had they but known it, the truth was in their favor. I keep *trying* to tell folk honesty is usually the best policy, but some fool folk just won't listen!"

He started to ask about the glue on the labels but decided it would be a waste of time. For however

Porter had done it, they had him if he wanted to make a fuss about it. If he didn't, they could do him as much damage by just having someone like old Bubbles spread the word in the purchasing office. Thinking of Bubbles reminded him he'd hardly be spending the night with poor Aurora, unless he wanted to act downright disgusting, and that the widow woman up to Sherman Avenue was likely to act mad as hell if he showed up after midnight again. So he thanked the lab man, who said not to mention it, and told Vail he was dying to get to work on his final report.

But as they were heading for the steps, further along the basement corridor Nurse Helen Healy caught up with them, looking rumpled as well as out of breath. She fell in step between them, saying, "Well, we've gotten things tidy again, no thanks to either of you naughty boys. Would someone please tell me, *now*, what all that excitement was about upstairs?"

Longarm slowed down to let Vail walk on as he told her, "It's your own fault for dashing in and out like that. You missed all the good parts. What time do you get off?"

She blinked up at him to reply, "I'm off at midnight. What has that got to do with you shooting up this hospital?"

He explained, "I got to run up to the Federal Building for an hour or so. I could get back in time to take you out for a late supper while I told you all about it, see?"

She dimpled but must have felt obliged to say, "I'm just bursting with curiosity, if it's understood that a late supper with you is as far as I might want to go."

183

He nodded, they shook on it, and sure enough, she was waiting there, dressed even prettier, when he showed up at midnight. But, somehow, he never got to finish his cleaned-up explanation of such a complicated case until they were having breakfast in bed the next morning.

Watch for

LONGARM AND THE OUTLAW SHERIFF

one hundred twenty-seventh novel in the bold
LONGARM series from Jove

coming in July!

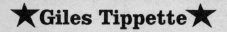